Blackbird
and
The Black Flower
Murders

ISBN-13: 978-0-9855495-2-7
eISBN: 978-0-9855495-3-4
Library of Congress Control Number: 2021909558
Beachbooks Entertainment, Inc.
Delray Beach, Florida
www.jelaine.co (co not com)

Blackbird
and
The Black Flower
Murders

J. E. Laine

MY NAME IS RITA

"So that's what you think I was talking about? That's what you think I meant?" I was pacing, sweating, my heart was pounding, my lips were quivering, my knees were shaking.

What does he think I meant by it. Does he think I love him? Yeah I love him. You can't cut a guy up like that if you don't love him. Anybody would know that. I like the way he bleeds, well of course it was helped by I cut him up in really pretty designs. To make the flow interesting, not just a pouring mess like some of them.

He can hardly talk anymore his voice is getting so weak, but it didn't gurgle yet. He's still saying things like why did I do it, he's crying now saying he doesn't want to die, and he's pleading for me to help him. But I can't, I just can't right now. I have things to do. Just bad timing some things.

Sometimes they get strange right about now, they know I could help them, really save their lives, they don't know how to act to me to convince me to help them and they can't believe that I'm concentrating on packing up and leaving. They should appreciate they got enough personal attention from me what am I their mother I should devote my life to them?

"Look," I said to Jeffrey. "I love you, that's what I mean don't you get it. And it's just enough now so good-bye. This is the new millennium." I wanted to sound profound, show that I was intelligent, not just some totally depraved and deprived nut. I had a good childhood, I went to college, but somewhere during the years I went crazy and I don't want anyone to know.

Goddamn it I just spent an hour carving those flowers on his chest, on his arms, oh and on his stomach they were incredible, especially when his belly would fill up and down with air while he was whimpering and it would look like the flowers were opening and closing, opening and closing. And then after all that what does he think I meant. I spent all this time I showed him how much I cared.

Nature is really incredible, isn't it. Look at all this stuff. Heads, hair, bones, Jesus Christ even little fingernails what didn't this god think of. I read that the toenails and fingernails keep growing for a long time after. When you're in your casket under the ground, in your crypt, in your mummification. And the hair too? The brain?

"Jeffrey, you need a haircut. I'll just give you a little trim before I leave. And your beard too." And then she left a note on a page ripped from the telephone book that said, "My name is Rita." She wrote it with a pen she found on the dresser. She took the pen.

Two days later she passed a newspaper stand and saw the headline Third Mutilated Body Found, thought about buying a copy but decided to wait till after lunch and kept walking.

RITA DREAMS

She kept telling the doctors about her dreams. They acted like the subject matter in her dreams was inconsequential. None of this was inconsequential, it was all that was happening to her, it inhabited her, it was her life.

Every night she tried to go to sleep, she really tried. She closed her eyes and counted all the fish that were trying to get away from the whale, and the ants that were trying to get to the glob of ice cream. After walking practically in circles, watching TV, trying to read, drinking warm milk, she would fall asleep and wake up six or seven times. And while she was asleep she would have a dream.

In one of them she was running down the hall, she heard the sound of footsteps and realized they were her own. Her back was sticky with sweat, she was sweating so much she could feel it dripping down her back, into her clothes. But her underarms, she thought, were dry, what kind of sweat was this she always sweated under her arms first, then everywhere else. She felt the sweat sopping down her sides coming out of her shirt. She looked down and saw her shirt was red, and when she wiped her nose with her sleeve it was red. She thought, "Oh. Okay. They found me." And the rest didn't have words to describe any of it, just the dark black night pulling on my wet hair, someone's teeth biting my lips and the fists keep punching me.

And then she didn't hear anything, she must have gotten away just in time before they killed her.

They never should have let her out. She woke up. She wanted this to stop. Why couldn't they just find her and take her back to the place. Those boys promised to protect me, they promised, but they just cared about themselves.

She bragged to anyone who would listen that she did a really good science project in Junior High one year, she carved the five senses in balsa wood with these great little sculpting knives, ten of them, each one had a different shaped blade but they all had a four and a half inch long rounded, just a little wider than a straw, wooden handle. One blade was wide curved like a graceful half moon, one was a tight U, one was V shaped, another was a straight piece of metal with a wide blade carved at a forty-five degree angle. There were slicers, scoopers, engravers, etchers, diggers. You see, it's the profile of the knife that shows you what design you will get. Some will dig deeper ditches than others, some shallow and straight, some medium and rounded.

In the movies they always use doctor's scalpels and sutures. But not me, she thought. I try to be as original as possible in all things. I had my set of little carving knives. My sculptures were so good they were on display in the school's glass trophy cabinet for years. There was the side view of the inside of the ear; I carved the anvil and the Eustachian canals. I carved the cross-section of the skin, the nose, the eyes. I even had little wires pretending they were hairs. Why didn't anyone call me to give them back? One day they were just gone.

I wasn't exactly shy or introspective, just when people were around. But when I walked down the street, they thought I was a movie star. Everybody would stare at me wondering what a big star like me was doing in their neighborhood.

One day, I knew, I'd be rich and then I

wouldn't have to figure anything out. I could go shopping all the time, I could travel and go to spas and I would never have to just sit there and think. I could control this thing.

DOUGLAS HEYWOOD

Terence Oliver straightened his perfectly tailored navy pin striped suit that was made for his extraordinarily well kept physique. He was shown into Douglas Heywood's sitting room by a uniformed butler whose pleasant deference befitted a servant. But Terence knew that anyone making the wrong move could be killed in seconds by this aide's bare hands. Such was the value of the person whose home he had just entered.

Heywood's house was built in the 1920's and looked like an enormous white cottage inn with more than forty forest green shingles eyelashing every window. Great lawns swelled from the front of the immense structure like golf courses without their balded mounds. It's back was nestled on a stretch of beach in one of Long Island's few private coves. Set on fifteen acres of property, which included forests, grand gardens, rolling hills and ponds, the house had every modern amenity, every high tech toy, and more than enough room to contain them.

He considered the meaning of Heywood's alarming telephone call. "Blackbird, Terence. Blackbird."

Blackbird. Death threat. The strong willed Heywood, for whom threats were not unusual, was uncharacteristically shaken by this one. Terence had avoided rush hour traffic to Great Neck by helicoptering over the Long Island Expressway and landing on Heywood's private heliport just two hundred yards east of the house.

"Would you care for something to drink while you wait for Mr. Heywood, sir?" the butler asked the visitor.

"Coffee will be fine, Charles," Terence said as he walked to the floor to ceiling window, it's curtains open and window slightly ajar to let in the refreshing spring day. It was only when Charles returned with the coffee and a tray of biscuits that he took a seat.

Of all the rooms in this incredible manse, he thought, this one had always been his favorite. It was the epitome of moneyed country house understatement. Mr. Heywood was one of the wealthiest men in the world, although you would never find this mentioned in Forbes or hear it in dinner conversation anywhere. Everything this man owned was the best, yet he was unpretentious about his riches. He had all the new toys but he wasn't showing off by having them. It's just that he invented the prototypes for most of them.

This room had several nestings of small couches, some in leather and some in Old World chintz florals, French white wood walls with paintings of charming country scenes and flower gardens, and a carpet whose color seemed an extension of the lawn outside.

For Terence, this room felt like life, while so much of his work reeked of the possibility of death. When he was left alone with his coffee to wait for his meeting to begin, he pondered Heywood's telephone call and extraordinary history.

He ran his hand through his thick blonde hair, took a sip of coffee and closed his eyes, which were green like the edge of a lake where the frogs play. "Blackbird. Oh shit," he thought out loud. Just when the political maneuvering and the international condition were in a welcomed balance, however tentative, he continued to himself.

It was not a secret within certain elite circles of the government that the death of Douglas Heywood would cause an international crisis. As the creator and navigator of the country's elaborate spy technological systems, he alone, outside of the highest officials, knew the procedures and codes that were used to inform the fate of the planet.

It would seem dangerous for any one individual to have garnered so much power but, in Heywood's case, his ascendancy was more a natural evolution of his unique talents and drive than intentional. His early genius and foresight were formidable; he had envisioned possibilities for the creation and improvement of high tech communications and detection equipment before anyone else. And he had an instinctually brilliant ability to build his complex inventions perfectly.

Insiders knew that his extraordinary talent had developed innocently. He could have been just another young boy playing with a toy walkie-talkie. But he had been exceptionally inquisitive. He had hungrily researched what information was available about such instruments. He processed what he learned, and then devised mechanical improvements. His models were faultless, and far beyond what was considered state of the art for the time. At the age of twenty he had confidently telephoned the New York office of the CIA, amazed every agent he met, and catapulted into the heady world of international affairs. From then on he was invaluable to the United States government.

Heywood's death would have a profound impact on the nation's security. He knew all the secrets. He had created most of them.

"Terence," said a voice from the entrance of the room, and Terence looked up with a start. Standing before him was the very statuesque and commanding Douglas Heywood, his visage, at first glance, belying not at all the strain his telephone call had suggested.

Terence sprang from his seat to shake hands. The two men, each a vigorous and handsome forty-five years old, had known each other for fifteen years through the most complicated global dynamics the world had ever known. Terence was, for many years, the highest ranking undercover courier in the nation, known only in this rarefied clandestine universe.

"My dear Terence," Heywood said graciously. His thick salt and pepper hair illuminated his strong cheekbones and twinkling brown eyes, and he strode eagerly towards his friend. "I'm so very pleased that you could come right away. Thank you." Terence heard the tension in the strained lower tones of his voice, and in the halting delivery of his words. He stood up, they shook hands and then hugged each other, as men often do when they have endured much together.

Terence remained standing and watched for hints of what was to come in Douglas Heywood's eyes. "You worried me, Douglas. It's not like you to sound panicked. Of course I'm here. Now tell me what's going on."

The two men sat across from each other on matching small forest green leather sofas as Heywood showed his friend and professional associate the note he had received.

> You took away our rightful respectful place in history. We must get it back and we must get back at you for this. In compensation for our suffering we will find a way to hurt you. There are so many choices. Your money, your life, your beautiful daughter, or something else. We will find a way.
> The Palacci

The rhythm and passion of the message was romantic in such a twisted way, Terence thought. He saw that Douglas Heywood's face turned pale as the walls as he took back the note and read it, doubtless for the several dozenth time.

"I've never heard of The Palacci, Douglas. Have you?"

"No. I haven't. But there are any number of leaders around the world who blame our country's high tech systems for their demise from power. And they're right, of course. But I didn't think that many knew that I personally created those systems."

"Only a few people on earth know. It was set up that way from the start. But we have always known that we can't be so naïve to think that others don't by now have both sophisticated systems and sources within our own government."

"Yes, of course. And there have always been threats directed towards me, but you've had no problem tracking them down. Not many of them seemed authentic. This one does. It has a terrifying sincerity."

Terence nodded, pursed his lips and slowly shook his head. "I've never known you to be afraid of anything or anybody, Douglas Heywood. And as much as I'd like to, I can't deny that I agree with you. This one does have a feeling of substance, and an intensely personal volcanic rage to it. You know I'll put everything we've got on it right away."

"The original is in the airtight container awaiting your office's inspection, Terence. Here, I've had a second copy of it made so that you could have one to probably reread as I have." Heywood took a folded note out of his inside breast pocket and handed it to Terence.

"How did you get the note, Terence? It didn't just land on your desk," said Cortland.

"Well actually, it almost did. When my secretary brought me my mail this morning, it was in a regular, white, number ten non-descript envelope. It seemed almost silly at first glance, and I might not have paid much attention, but the same note was in three other letters, written in different type on different kinds of paper. I have kept all in the safe for you."

"We have to find out where this threat is coming from, Terence," Heywood implored. "You know that I can handle the most intricate and frightening threats to civilization, I can track anything or anybody in the world to protect this country. But I cannot deal with threats that might involve Samantha."

It was well known among Heywood's intimate acquaintances that he doted on his beautiful daughter. Anyone who took the time to examine his life would easily know that she was his most obvious weakness. But until this moment it had seemed unimaginable that anyone would use that knowledge as if it were a stock tip, even in the world of intrigue that he lived in. Indeed, most civilized regimes left women and children out of their political strategies, except for those that kept them subservient, and therefore powerless.

Terence stood up. "Douglas. This country owes you, and this will be taken care of. Where is Samantha now?"

Heywood's eyes focused on a picture of Samantha in a silver frame on the end table to his left. "She's just finished her year in France, and she planned on spending the next few months at home with Lyla and I." He moved his eyes towards Terence, who thought that Heywood looked like he had aged in the last few minutes, his usually powerful voice sounded sad. "We've missed her, but spending real time abroad, and on her own, so to speak, was something we had promised her. She's always shown a remarkable talent for my work and she's wanted to get involved. As you know, I've tried to dissuade her, not because she's a woman, but because of risks like this. She's too young and too beautiful to have such serious weights on her shoulder. Or perhaps I've been too protective a father." The last was as much a question as a statement.

"She's an exceptional, intelligent woman. If she wasn't your daughter, I have no doubt that you would have harnessed her talents within your organization already."

"You're probably right. But she is my daughter, and now that she's back, I want her to have as normal a life as possible for as long as possible. I certainly don't want her to feel like a prisoner here.

But now she'll have to have security guards, however discreet, wherever she goes. And I'll have to put limits on her movements."

"You're right. That won't be avoidable for awhile," Terence said. "Let me get to the office and look into this. I'll phone you later today. And look, this might turn out to be just another one of those idle threats, you know?"

Terence's attempt at levity hadn't worked for either of them. They looked at each other, both sensing that they were about to enter a nightmare that could easily spiral out of control.

GRETA MEETING

The sixth car had just pulled into the parking area located on the west side of the estate's red brick mansion. All of the cars were American made and nondescript in basic beiges, grey and black. By 9 a.m. each of the car's drivers had walked through the grove of trees that surrounded the house, opened the massive oak doors with a special key, and had taken their established seats around the imposing rectangle jade green marble table in the dining room.

A seventh man, the eldest, sat at the head of the table wearing a formal pewter hued morning suit. His large gray eyes shimmered like well polished silver, and they were beautifully similar in color to his generous head of hair. He nodded to each man as they took their places, and the scene might have been an innocuous gathering of friends except that, when he spoke, his eyes became unmercifully calculating and cold.

"Gentlemen, thank you for joining me this morning," he began.

"Good morning, Mr. G," the group responded in manly dissonant tones.

"I've asked you here this morning because we have a new mission." The room was silent except for the inaudible sighs that he knew begged to be whispered from each in his audience.

And so he said, "I understand. But please, have coffee and something to eat while I tell you the generalities. Then we will have a full breakfast after which, as usual, we will undertake the details."

Next to each man were the same items provided when their meeting took place at this time of day: a sterling silver thermos of hot coffee, a Limoges set of creamer, sugar bowl, cup and saucer all bearing a golden orb circled with a gold and silver ring, the same logo that was on the white linen napkins, sterling silverware and serving pieces. Each setting had a woven silver basket of breakfast rolls and a china tray of fresh raspberries, cream, jellies and preserves.

"But sir," responded one of the six newly arrived men. "I thought we were going to disband after the last assignment."

"You're quite right, of course. But between the world's current configuration and a new turn of events, which is the subject of our meeting, that is no longer possible."

Seated around the table were Ainsley, Brenner, Cortland, Dennis, Eton, Farlow and the stealth society's leader Garrison, known unceremoniously as Mr. G. When the organization was created, just after World War II, it had been only by coincidence that each of the seven senior members' names began with one of the first seven letters of the alphabet. All of their successors resolved to maintain that tradition, even if it meant using a middle or a last name and, without exception, that mandate was always accomplished. Amid the strict codes of obligations, performance and conduct, they deserved that one agenda that was frivolous, however efficient. The rest were always a matter of survival.

Each man had been hand picked from thousands of scrupulously researched possibilities, all had been distinguished in a necessary field, and all had been deemed absolutely qualified and trustworthy. GRETA, Global Reconnaissance Elite Tactical

Agents, had been established later than the other intelligence departments of the United States government. The only difference between the government's intelligence communities and this one was that GRETA's existence was hidden from the public, and it was accountable to no formally recognized jurisdiction. In other words, GRETA did not officially exist. Except that it had once been sanctioned by the government but never governed by the government, and so it received certain benefits while maintaining its absolute autonomy. A reality that found certain frustrated politicians trying to squash regularly.

Within the organization only Mr. G knew who had operational authority over the organization. The senior men knew only that it was certainly not the public, but nor was it within the auspices of any recognized branch of government. Most assumed for a while that it was the government. After that, they knew that they were involved in something that would more justly and insistently uphold what was morally and ethically right in the world than a reigning government might, as it was too often swayed by politics and party needs.

To assure the group's perpetuation there was a functional hierarchy beneath the sitting prestigious group, although the future heirs to this elite corps had no idea who was training them, or for what they were ultimately being prepared.

The senior men of GRETA poured their coffee and listened. While all were apprised of every GRETA mission, only three were designated as operational for each mission while the others were held in reserve, just in case, and kept abreast of all necessary details. The three chosen for this assignment were Brenner, Cortland and Farlow. Seven hours later, all but one senior GRETA had left the estate.

Mr. G walked into the study and pushed a button that opened a two foot square section of the walnut paneled walls. On the screen that was now before him he could see an aerial view of the property.

He watched as infra red beams swept every inch of the grounds. When he was certain that the next to last car and driver had left the estate, he sat in the gold brocade cushioned chair at the mahogany desk which was edged with a ring of dark brown leather inlays. He unlocked the right hand drawer, pressed three numbers on the telephone pad and picked up the receiver. "You can come into the study now," he said.

When Terence Oliver walked into the room Mr. G continued. "As you heard, I've set the wheels in motion. Within the next few days we'll be in the muck and mire with this, you know. Whoever threatened Douglas Heywood had better know how to hide."

"Thank you, Garrison."

"Please. Sit down."

"There's no time for that today," Terence said calmly.

"Will you at least tell me why you won't discuss this with the President?"

"I'm sorry. No. At least not now."

"I understand," Garrison said matter-of-factly.

"I would hope that you do."

"I also understand that you might never be able to tell me."

"It's for your own safety. You know that."

Garrison sat back in his chair and took a deep breath, then let the air out slowly. "Do you think things will ever change?"

"Are you getting tired, old man?" Terence responded with a warm twinkle in his eyes.

"Not so many years ago, I would have been devastated to hear you ask that. Now, I admit, I wouldn't mind the rest."

"You've worked hard. You've devoted most of your life to GRETA."

"If we've accomplished what we set out to do, it will have been worth it."

"You're the only one who's had the genius to oversee it properly. We still haven't found anyone who could possibly replace you."

"Thank you, Terence. But, as tired as I am, I'm not quite ready to step down yet," Garrison said as he looked reflectively around the room.

"And we wouldn't want you to. I have to leave now." When Terence reached the study door, he turned around. "When this mission is over and resolved, it will be your finest hour, you know."

"And if it's not resolved..."

"It will be our country's worst nightmare."

SAND

The last time Cortland was on a beach, they had made love. But Amy, the finally found love of his life, had disappeared. His tortured mind knew that he had to stop thinking about her and concentrate only on his survival. He had endured far worse than this in his work with GRETA, but this was now and now required his full concentration.

Twenty feet to his left were the dunes that would hide him if he could get to their other side. But the way the moonlight sporadically hit them, he risked being spotted on their crests. Straight ahead, about twenty yards, were bushes and trees that would give him cover and maybe even something to eat. Would they hear him crawling through the thicket of thorny bramble and dried reeds? Just a few days ago he had been selfishly thrilled with the two month draught. He and Amy liked to make love on a blanket of sand and nature's dried beach swill under the stars. Now he knew the parched sounds could cause his death. The men were no more than two hundred feet to his right, he could see their silhouettes and their lighted cigarettes. He had no choice.

He was tired and hungry, and the z pattern he made on the sand made his trip more than twice as long as it had to be but this was the way he had been trained. If he was spotted, it would be harder to shoot at him if he wasn't moving in a straight line. What was it that Brenner always said? Slither like a snake, spring like a rabbit and run like a jaguar.

He was ten miles north of the Florida Everglades on a plot of beach bordering secret government owned land that several major corporations and developers were bidding on. He was miles from inhabited land, and the hot humid tropical air made him feel like his body was coated with honey.

The sand was so dry and loose he could crawl into it if he needed quick cover, he thought, but so far the bastards seemed to have forgotten to bring a flashlight. The gun was bruising his hip, and the knife that was strapped to his leg moved off the leather strip and was gnawing at him mercilessly. Good god what had he done to deserve this life, he thought.

He wormed his way into the bushes for about fifteen feet and leaned against the trunk of a tree. It was the first time that he had allowed his body to stop in a few hours, but his mind continued to race. He grabbed some berries that were hanging in front of his face and stuffed them into his mouth. Then he took off his khaki jacket and pulled the tan Izod tee shirt over his head and then he ripped it, slowly and quietly, into strips. He removed the knife from its strap and used a few pieces of the shirt fabric to soak up the blood on his leg. He reached for an aloe stem, peeled several leaves and rubbed their salve into his wounds. Then he tied three strips of fabric around his calf and pulled his tan chino pants leg back down.

From where he sat in the bushes he could still see the figures of the three men scanning the beach and the horizon. At that moment, one of them left the group and started walking towards the ocean. There were enough clouds in the sky to render this night dark and dismal except for a few moon rays that snuck through only now and then. Hopefully they wouldn't see his tracks.

The one who had walked on the beach yelled back to his compatriots, "He's nowhere the fuck around here. Must'a dove into the ocean and swam to China. Where's goddamn Lou with the flashlights, god damn it?"

Then Cortland heard it. It was still far away, but there was no mistaking the sound of a chopper. It was flying without lights cruising the shoreline looking for him. Brenner always came through, he thought, but unless these assholes left the beach, his friend would never use headlights to find him and put both of their lives in jeopardy. Damn. Then there was the sound of another engine, but this one was much closer. It was a truck with blaring headlights speeding towards the men who wanted to kill him.

He wanted to signal Brenner, but he couldn't draw attention to himself without risking getting shot. There was no way, unless he could divert the goons' attention. He knew Brenner understood what was going on as he watched the truck's headlights, and how the three men were racing around the beach with their just arrived flashlights. If Brenner tried to land he'd get bullet holes in his copter, or worse. Surely the men were about to see his tracks in the sand. He was on his own. He prepared himself for an attack.

The noise of the whirlybird faded away. Damn, he's giving up, Cortland thought. He's leaving me here with these idiots. Then he smiled. Less than a quarter of a mile down the beach there was a series of loud bursts that sounded like gun shots. And then some more. Within moments the three men that were hunting him down were screaming at each other and running for their car.

Brenner did it after all, he chuckled to himself. He had thrown a few canisters of the ammo they had rigged up to timers. Sounded like a real gun fight. Within a few minutes his would-be predators were gone.

Cortland ran onto the beach and pulled a flare from his jacket pocket. He popped an orange one and within moments Brenner was hovering over him hoisting him up to safety. As his foot grabbed onto the second rung of the rope ladder, a shot flew by his head, and then another one careened off the side of the heavily armored bird. Cortland held on for dear life as Brenner maneuvered the craft just out of gunshot.

"Thanks, pal," Cortland panted as he pulled his body into the flying cab. "I thought they all left. Guess they deserve more credit than I've given them."

Brenner swerved the chopper over the water and then veered inland. "The truck's moving fast. But shit. We lost the car. They must have driven into some foliage and turned off the lights."

"Let's drop this bucket and shake the truck driver down. I want to find that bastard. We have got to solve this mission, sooner rather than later. And any lead is a goddamn lead," Cortland said as he quickly replaced the cloths on his bloody leg after he applied an antibiotic ointment and gauze. Then he put on a clean shirt from the supply box.

"They could be on foot ready to ambush us, you know," Brenner replied.

"Good. We'll make them have a little chat with us." Jim Cortland spoke with a confidence that only fifteen years of using his body as a lethal weapon could give him. "By the way, how the hell did you find me?"

"I figured you'd be near the water, Cortland. First tell me what happened down there and then I'll tell you what's shaking on my end."

"No news about Amy, I guess."

"No. Nothing yet, pal. Sorry."

Cortland pulled in all the air he could hold, turned away from his friend and screamed, "those fucking scum bags." Then he took a few deep breaths and said, "Well then, I've got another priority right now. Got any food aboard?"

"Just happen to have a roast beef on rye and a can of apple juice, pal."

As Cortland attacked his sandwich, he filled his partner in. Then he said, "I don't know where he gets all of his hired hands, Brenner. They're a different bunch wherever we go. Makes it impossible to know who we're tracking. But we'll find the son of a bitch behind it all. I know we will."

Brenner put on his headlights as he hovered over the truck. They watched the vehicle swerve in panic below them. "I see a nice patch. We'll slip in right there," he said as he aimed the craft towards the small clearing. "Down we go," Brenner sang.

The two men drew their guns and ran from the darkened helicopter into the bushes. It was eerily quiet. Then a shot rang out but missed them both by far. They nodded to each other and split up, Cortland to the left, Brenner to the right. Cortland saw the lone man first, crouching behind a bush, pointing his gun at nothing. He silently inched his way through the bushes and threw a rock to his far left to divert the man's gaze. Then he pounced. He hit the man over the head with the barrel of his gun just hard enough to knock him out for awhile. Then he whistled, one short bird like note, so that Brenner would know where he was and that he had caught someone.

When Brenner reached him Cortland whispered, "Let's wrap this one up. He's got to be Lou. He's the one who was bringing the other guys flashlights."

Brenner pulled rope from his pants and tied Lou's hands behind his back. Then he tied his feet, taped his mouth, and stuffed the gun Lou dropped into his own waistband. They both heard the footsteps of the other three men carelessly and noisily running in their direction.

"Wait here," Cortland said with a smirk on his face. He stood still until he was sure he knew where the scampering footsteps were coming from. He crouched so that his head would be below the line of the bushes and stealthily followed the sounds. Then he heard their muffled voices.

"They must'a found Lou by now," one of them said. "That dumb guy probably shit in his pants. He better not talk. We were stupid to call him. He doesn't know the rules."

"Shut up, Frank," the second man said in as low a voice as he could achieve.

"What do ya mean sayin shut up to me Vinnie?" Frank shot back.

"Keep your voice down, you know Frank? They're gonna hear us. And so if Lou talks, what's he gonna say, anyway. He don't know anyone's real name except Sal here, and Sal's good at pretending he don't know nothin, ain't you Sal?"

"Yeah boss. You know I am."

Vinnie looked at the two men and said in a cold monotone, "Now, we got a job to do. Let's find those whirlybird boys and break their fuckin necks."

Just as Vinnie said 'necks,' a foot shot up from the bushes, slammed him in the throat and knocked him, back down, onto the ground.

"What the...," and Frank got a hand slice in his solar plexus and a jab to the back of his head. Cortland swirled to his right, said, "Hiya Sal," and slam-dunked him to the ground.

Cortland heard a sound coming from his left and he spun around again. "Good timing again, Brenner. Let's tie these guys up tight and put'em all on board."

"Nice work, Cortland. What do you want to do with them?" Brenner asked, as if he didn't know the answer.

"Let's take them to the cave."

THE CAVE

The Cave had been used by GRETA and the United States government for over forty years variously as a top secret meeting place for undercover assets, a safe house, a research site, a storage facility for special classified materials, interrogation headquarters and temporary prison for special guests.

Of course it wasn't a cave at all, although it's nickname by all who knew of it was apt. The three story structure had been built underground using similar theories of physics as the Lincoln and Holland tunnels in New York. Burrowed deeper into the earth, its' construction was built to be bomb, radiation, hurricane, water, chemical, earthquake and volcano proof. Most importantly, it was detection and penetration proof.

The cave's ground cover and hidden entrances were impossible to reach by anyone who didn't have the highly select Code K219 rating. The constellation's perimeter was encircled by tall barbed wire tipped aluminum fence with signs saying Federal Government Property Keep Out. If the fence was approached to within three feet, a calmly forceful warning would be issued by an imperturbable computerized voice that said, "You are ordered to leave this government perimeter immediately." If the trespassers remained there for more than forty-five seconds, they were treated to brief but significant rushes of electricity.

For those who braved the fence, whether innocent pranksters or true marauders, the interlopers were in for a minor life altering experience. Once on the compound's grounds, they would be subjected to the land's dynamic fabrication. The complex was ringed by concentric circles of above and underground electronic sound sensors and tiny periscopic cameras that were embedded in filaments and cables that coiled for two miles. Any sensory fluctuation was measured and imaged instantaneously.

The trespassing body would be inoculated with a paralyzing chemical that would allow agents to carry the torso into the compound for later interrogation. Harmless intruders were returned to society with, at the least, a meaningful memory loss. Menacing intruders were treated to the cave's various hospitalities.

The fortress could not be detected from the ground or by air, as it was camouflaged artfully by the waters, flower and fauna indigenous to the area. Neither could the structure be detected by sonar, radar or any other high capability detection system that had yet been devised by man. The cave was coated with an invincible, highly classified, manmade compound that had been the brainchild of Douglas Heywood.

The facility's coating was made of a lethal radiation bearing microorganism which had been infested into an ordinary polyvinyl chloride resin. That preparation was mixed with the residue from the burning of a newly discovered element, code named Pyron. The combined mixture formed an incredible dual acting substance. The layer of the compound that touched the surface of the building's skin hardened, while the upper layers, even with tons of earth and sea over it, became a gaseous envelope whose molecules covered the structure seemingly barely attached but suspended, like trillions of helium balloons tethered by strings, to the solid surface. The result was an inert, impregnable and virtually undetectable solution.

For reasons essential to the national security, not even the military had been informed of this futuristic compound, although it could have been used to create stealth ships, aircraft and military installations. The government knew that all it took was one greedy informer, and the invaluable substance could be shopped internationally and sold to the highest bidder, most certainly to a country hostile to the United States.

Incredible precautions had been taken with the men who had been recruited to build the structure. They never knew exactly where they were or what they were working on, so complete was the shroud of secrecy surrounding the site's existence. The construction was performed in carefully calibrated increments to avoid any cohesive comprehension of the project outside of each man's own purposefully limited scope. Deliveries of materials were split into delivery cells. Some men were voluntarily temporarily blinded prior to being led inside to then detail their construction expertise. Except for the cave's creators, only the operatives involved in the project's end, the high tech wizards who tied all of the pieces together, knew what it was.

With satellites more numerous than any one branch of it's own nation knew about, the cave photographed and tapped into intelligence information from all over the world. It ingested the data, and, through its super computers and infinity networks, it sorted, sifted, and made sense of all that the insatiable machinery digested. And then, like the fiery bellowing of a great thundering reptile, the facility spun out reams of intelligence and counter intelligence information that formed much of the world's political comprehension of itself. No one had been able to trace the location or source of this intelligence power. Nor had anyone, other than its inventor, Douglas Heywood, even envisioned the instruments that were capable of such command.

Entering the cave required negotiating an intricate system of codes, colors, holograms, infra black showers and instant DNA signatures. Two of the entrances could be reached from the ground, and one entrance required a dive beneath the sea, where the cave was entered like a submarine. Not counting 'guests,' there were never more than some dozens of Code K219 authorizations assigned at any time.

Once inside, it took the uninitiated a long time to behold and grasp the unimaginable sight before them. All but one of the cave's three entrances lead into the main room, referred to informally as the reception area. The reception area procedures were determined by the visitor's status and objective. It was an enormous white marbled floored room, with five alcoves radiating from it. The alcoves were actually the beginnings of long passageways that spread from the main room like the overstuffed tendrils of a fat octopus.

Each of the five corridors had a purpose, some a multi-purpose, and access to each tendril was possible only by a series of complex codes and methods of identification. In general, the first corridor was the most benign. It contained the living quarters, sleeping rooms, suites for dignitaries, lounges, the kitchens and dining rooms. The second wing was for special meetings and conferences, the third housed research and storage facilities, the fourth was for interrogations and prisoners. Only a few people in the world knew what was in the fifth passageway.

Cortland knew what was in the fifth corridor.

Cortland and Brenner had drugged their four captives Lou, Frank, Vinnie and Sal and locked them into separate and isolated cells deep in the bowels of the cave. The hostages didn't know if they were waiting for their interrogations or their executions. And, as the men from GRETA knew, the longer they were kept waiting, the more frightened they would become, and the more apt they were to talk. So they let them wait.

The cave was like a country club for the

world's most elite spooks. It was one of the few places on the planet where one could speak freely without fear of being overheard by the wrong element. Every room was continuously swept, every telephone line and communication system was secure, and anyone in the common sectors of the cave had top priority clearances. In case of war on American shores, the president could run the U.S. government from here.

Cortland and Brenner showered and then met, as planned, in one of the lounges to have coffee. "Even if these goons talk," Brenner said to Cortland, "they're only intermediaries. They'll know nothing, pal. I was sort of surprised that you wanted to bring them here."

"But I knew you understood. If it weren't for Amy's disappearance, I probably wouldn't have. But I'll ply anyone we grab on this mission with terror, and talking juice if I have to, whatever it takes, until we get even one word that leads us to something. Right now we have nothing, unless there are some new developments I don't know about. Are there?"

"Not much I'm afraid."

"Well, let's hear it while we can sit still for a change and shoot some of this caffeine into our veins."

They sat back comfortably.

"I'm just so fuckin tired," continued Cortland. And I'm worried about Amy. Somehow she's been thrown into this." Cortland looked off into the distance at nothing, and then he snapped back into the skilled analyst warrior that he was trained to be. "Let's hear it."

"Look pal. I know regulations say I gotta talk about the mission first, but let me tell you what I know about Amy."

"Regulations don't have to tell me that these are not two different situations. I don't have the proof yet, but I know it. And in this business, knowing is the proof. But it's all right, Brenner. Let's cover the mission first."

"As you know, this is Force One Alert.

Farlow's our source point. All communications go through him. All international assets have been notified. They know you're following your own leads, but they're getting nibbles from Europe and they need you on line with them. You're their favorite son, Cortland. There's nobody they trust more than you."

"Aren't I lucky."

"Of course you're lucky. But more than that, you're brilliant."

"And there's no better enforcer than you, and they know that. That's why I always insist on your being my adjunct. They know I won't do a Force One with anyone else."

"There's more. But they'll only fill you in when you reach Farlow."

"Okay. Now tell me about Amy."

"They put a non-GRETA on that. You know, Mark Stevens, from FBI. And, of course, he's not cleared to know everything you know."

"They're misusing manpower here. If they know I'm so brilliant, why the hell aren't they listening to me?" The veins in Cortland's neck were engorged. "The timing of her disappearance isn't a god damn coincidence. I know it has something to do with the threat on Douglas Heywood. What makes them so sure that these are unrelated incidences?"

"I don't know, but they have sources that we don't have. And anyway, maybe everything will be clarified when you speak to Farlow today."

"It's so obvious. They threaten to kidnap Heywood's daughter Samantha. But he's got her hidden. Somehow they identify me and kidnap my girlfriend. To show they're serious. To show that nothing is going to stop them. To show they're getting closer."

"How could they identify you?"

"Brenner, I don't know that, but I do know that we don't even know who *they* are. Damn them! Get back to Steven's watch on Amy."

"He's on the alert twenty-four hours a day no

matter what. All he's got so far is that her neighbor saw her leave her house on her bicycle at 10 a.m. Tuesday morning. Her basket was empty and she was heading towards the market down the road where she always buys her fresh produce. The man at the market says he never saw her that day. The neighbor says that was the last time he saw her. He was home all day. He says he always knows when she's home cause he hears the music she keeps on when she's there."

"Yeah. She loves to listen to all those crooners. Sinatra's her favorite, but she listens to all of them. She's got a year's worth of tapes and CDs."

The frustration and helplessness Cortland felt lifted him off his chair. He knew that the only way he could make sure that things happened was by making them happen. He was half way to the door when he turned to Brenner and said, "I gotta get on the phones. See if you can find out who else is here today, will you Brenner? I'll meet you in twenty minutes in the Command Lounge. Then we'll see if our little jailbirds know anything."

Cortland made a quick detour to retrieve a small package from his locker, which was actually a secured vault that only he had access to. Then he worked his way through the labyrinth of corridors and check points until he reached the Section B Communications room.

He strode into the room and requisitioned unrestricted access to all systems without delay, which his priority rank delivered. He was quickly ushered into a private room, and within moments he was sitting behind an elaborate console. As he entered the codes that would project Farlow onto a one-way screen, he carefully stripped the package on his lap of its heavily padded leather case.

He had in his possession one of the world's few audio visual telepathic monitors, called a Sensory Imagery Validator, or SIV, which onomatopoeic Cortland thought most fitting. He inserted its cable into a special adapter and plugged it into the console. With a flick of a switch he was able not only to see and hear Farlow, he could discern, from color patterns fluttering on the screen, every nuanced affectation of his colleague's moods. As a member of GRETA, Farlow, like Cortland and Brenner, was cleared beyond the confines of the government's established intelligence domain. But not for an SIV. Cortland intended to become proficient with his new toy, and therefore used it, and experimented with it, whenever possible. Besides, no matter how thorough the clearing procedures and how absolute the results, there were few people that Cortland trusted unconditionally.

When the equipment confirmed Cortland's DNA and digital signatures, Farlow's image came into immediate focus on the screen. Deemed one of the world's most brilliant intelligence analysts, he was clearly unprepared for his television debut of the day. His football hero sized torso was slouched over his desk, and strands of his disheveled black hair had fallen over his jet brown eyes in such a way that it looked like his face was behind bars. On Cortland's SIV screen Farlow's head was surrounded by calming shades of blue, which indicated that he was at least resting. But there were flickers of red in his cerebral region which represented intense cognitive activity.

"Yo Farlow. Are you in one of your analysis driven trances mate?"

As Farlow started talking, his head and body elongated to an upright position. "Cortland, you uninvited prick," he muttered as his Olympic proportions stretched onto the screen. "Can't a man rest in peace in the privacy of his own little office cubicle?" His feigned anger was undermined by a good-natured smile. "I'm putting an end to all future spy toys, unless I can have one too, of course." Then he got serious. "What's going on, Cortland?"

Cortland knew that Farlow hadn't been briefed yet about the SIV, so he ignored what might have been a serious breach of engagement. He understood that Farlow was just chitchatting, as was his tendency when he wasn't practicing his formal methodology. "Brenner and I brought a few men to the cave with us. I don't think we'll get much from them."

"You were good out there, Cortland. Your little run across the beach will make a great training movie for sand crabs."

"Well, I thank our heavenly satellites for supplying you with your adventure show for the day. I take that to mean that you have nothing to add at this time. And remember, now it's my turn to beam you in. Sorry but I'm in a secure room, so it's not reciprocal."

Cortland watched as Farlow's immense hands gripped a coffee mug and brought it to his mouth for a quick gulp. His body became rigid, and his face suddenly bore the expression that had earned him his renown. When Farlow was about to impart his knowledge, the attitude of his body suggested that he was nothing less than a living breathing computer. His sharp gaze penetrated the distance and technology between them to such a degree that Cortland was riveted to the screen.

"Listen closely," Farlow began, his voice deep, clear and monotone. "Your enemy is a large man who rules a small kingdom. He is not as bright as we are, nor does he have anything near our resources. His fury is profound, but its dynamic is one of frantic desperation. It's emotionally rather than intelligently driven. Which makes it easy for us on one level. But on another level, it makes our work, your work, far more dangerous. He has the potential to out maneuver us, and for possibly a long time. But because he is emotionally driven, he will, at some point, mess up."

Cortland assumed Farlow's report was correct. It always was. Because the intensity in Farlow's eyes hadn't changed, he assumed there was more.

"But we don't yet know if he's head of a country, a city, a corporation or his own domain. Or what part of the world he is in."

"But the note..."

"Anybody can get an American to translate anything into Americanese and make it sound like it's your cousin. You know better than that."

"Does Mr. G have any leads for me, assuming my four captives prove as useless as I think they will?"

"He'll contact you tonight."

Cortland noticed that the red activity in Farlow's brain sprouted what looked like little yellow torches.

"What is it Farlow?"

The automaton looked at a piece of paper on his desk and blushed. "This is not within the realm of our mandate." He looked around, as might a young schoolboy who thought he was doing something naughty. "But tell me," he whispered, "your thoughts about your ah...ah...your friend. The lady. Amy." Farlow's face was crimson.

It was known in GRETA that Farlow's life, while not totally devoid of meaningful human relationships, favored processing the modus operandi of people and situations with his gadgetry world of techno connections rather than with his heart.

"I know that Amy's kidnapping is related to our mission, Farlow. I don't know why that investigation is being conducted separately. Do you?"

Farlow's stare was momentarily blank, his colors blue, followed by a wash of red and yellow. Clearly the question had been thoroughly examined. "No," he said. "I don't know why."

Cortland paused for a moment before he spoke. "Thank you. I appreciate your concern. If you think of anything please let me know. And if you can help me convince Mr. G to combine the investigations..."

"Your emotionality would be a detriment. I think that is what he is trying to transcend. You have never been observed functioning in a potentially emotionally impaired condition. That is not how you are known here. I believe that is his fear. Do you concur?"

"I'm not sure. I'm leaving now. Thank you again."

He entered the codes for FBI operative Mark Stevens, but the signal that came back to him indicated that Stevens was unavailable. Cortland knew that Stevens would not know about the cave or about GRETA. In fact, he had been advised that Cortland was functioning only within the FBI. He left his generic coded message, sort of an email for secret agents, that did not have to include locations. He packed up the SIV and left word with the Command Lounge Chief for Brenner to meet him in the prison reception hall.

Two hours later they were completing the interrogation of their third hostage. The first two knew nothing. This one, Sal, cared only about saving his own life. If he couldn't get home alive, he was ready to work for Cortland or Brenner. When he said, "If I learn the lingo of your vocabulary, can I be in your profession, man?" Cortland said, "go fuck yourself," punched him in the face and pulled Brenner out of the room.

"This guy is too stupid to be deep cover for anything," Cortland exhaled.

"One more to go." Brenner glanced at his partner. "You look really beat."

"I am," Cortland replied.

Vinnie, their last charge, carried out his macho bravura for far longer than had Sal, Frank and Lou. He was clearly petrified. When Brenner grabbed his crotch and threatened to have his testicles removed, the trembling man cried for the lord and for every person in his family. When it seemed that Brenner was ready to summon the dismemberment surgeon, Vinnie screamed that his instructions had come from a man in New York, which information Cortland immediately wired to Mr. G.

THE BEACH

The only thing that a man could want that wasn't provided for him in the cave was a woman. And the only woman that Jim Cortland wanted was Amy. Unimaginably, Amy had disappeared.

He hadn't worried much about it when he hadn't heard from her for a day. She was a writer and liked to go off by herself to work on story lines. But she had never lost touch for more than a day. After two days of not hearing from her, he had known something was wrong.

He agonized over what she might be going through, and reviewed in his mind, over and over again, all of the things he had not told her. To protect her. Now he knew that just knowing him had put her life in jeopardy.

He tried to think of something else, anything else, so that he could get the sleep he so desperately needed. But alone in bed in a dark room he was suddenly aware only of the ache in his loins. He had showered the sand and sweat from his body, and had watched as little mounds of sand formed on the bath tiles. He hadn't been ready then, but now he let himself think of the memories the sight of those little mounds of sand had unlocked. The first day he met Amy they had made love in the ocean, and when they showered in his house, sand had coated the shower tiles. He grabbed his penis and relived every detail of that day.

She was long and tan and beautiful, with blonde hair draping seductively around her head and flowing off the sides of the beach blanket. Her body was greased and shiny with suntan lotion. Any healthy male would stop in his tracks to take in this fantastic sight, Cortland had thought as his feet burned in the scorching sand, while nevertheless he stood still and stared. For an instant he looked down at his own body, gratefully noting that he still had his loose Bermuda shorts over his tight bathing suit. Very few episodes were more embarrassing than growing a bulge in luminous blue lycra. He remembered that, in his teens, such was almost always the case. Then too in his youth he had never had the nerve to start a conversation with any of the girls he had been attracted to and learned, all too painfully, that a moment lost is a moment gone. So he walked over to her.

Cortland took a deep breath and said the first thing that came to his mind, "What's your name?"

She didn't flinch or skip a beat. She said, "Amy." And then, without taking off her eye protectors, she asked, "And what's your name?"

As he answered, "Cortland," she removed her plastic goggles, opened her eyes and started to turn her body over and around to face the direction of his voice. He noticed that her ass was as voluptuous as the front of her. He wanted to slide all over her oily skin before she said another word. But he, of course, would not do that. She brushed the hair and some sand from her face, and squinted up at him with pale blue eyes that reminded him of his grandmother's lapis ring.

"I'm not sure what to say now," he continued. "I only know that I had to talk to you. I don't know about you, but I've let too many chances in my life slip away, only to regret them later. I didn't want to add another, and a very avoidable one, to that list."

Her head cocked, first to the left, and then to the right. She knew how attractive she was. The many obnoxious ways men had approached her over the years had become routine and boring. Most tried transparently to be subtle, and most failed. But this man seemed different. His sincerity was convincing and resourceful. She was curious.

"Would you care to join me for a little while?" she offered, giving herself the out in case her first impressions of him did not withstand a real attempt at the kind of communication she liked. She certainly could not lose face or risk danger on this crowded seashore.

"Amy," he sighed with a hoarseness in his voice he could not help. He took a deep breath and continued, "Let's get past my telling you how very beautiful and enticing you are. I'm sure you're sick of hearing that."

"I've never minded hearing it at the appropriate time and for the right reason," she said as she sat up to face him. "But if you're implying that I'm tired of hearing it as a come-on and a line, you're absolutely right. And I appreciate your acknowledging that. But let's be honest, shall we? Unless we've met on the telephone or through letters, there is only each other's physical appearance to absorb. Everything else follows." She looked at him admiringly, then added, "And, to get us completely past that stage, I'll admit that I find you most attractive."

He smiled, his azure green eyes twinkling at her. "I'm relieved to hear you say that. Our relationship might have just ended if you didn't feel that way." He looked down at her blanket, then in her eyes and said, "And I would have been sulking right now instead of trying to come up with an original way to find out more about you."

She smiled back at him and suggested, "Let's take turns asking each other questions."

"Fair enough. Tell me about you, what you do with your life, where you come from. I don't mean to sound like a glutton, but I want to know everything about you." In fact, he thought, he had never felt quite like this. He had never been so interested in the details of a woman's life.

"That was more than one question," she paused, deciding whether or not to go on. "Well all right. I'd like to say something very impressive like I'm in the midst of a very constructive and creative phase of my life, but I'm not. I write for magazines, I've just started my first book and I travel a lot. But right now I'm living in parenthesis."

"You're uh, living where?"

"I'm in between things. I was quite involved with a number of projects, but I'm simply not doing much of anything right now." She looked at him and smiled, and he noticed for the first time how her dimples seemed to sparkle. "I'll be honest with you. I love it. I absolutely love having nothing in particular to do. I've never done this before, done not much, that is. It's like a gift of time that I'm giving to myself."

"I see. It sounds like you're very happy."

"I am very happy. Now it's my turn, and I get two plus questions. Who are you, and what do you do?"

"That was fast. You didn't give me much lead time to prepare. I thought you were going to go into a bit more detail about yourself." Cortland squinted his eyes and looked thoughtfully at Amy, who waited expectantly for his answer, so he continued. "I do a little international work for the government, and I also travel quite often."

"What kind of work for the government? And where do you travel?"

"Whatever they need me to do at any given time, and wherever that is."

"You could be asked to do anything, anywhere in the world?"

"Yes. That's right."

"Intelligence?"

"I'd like to think so." They both smiled, then laughed, their first laugh together. "I suppose you could call it that," he continued.

"I see." She picked up her bottle of suntan lotion and began to spread the bronze goo on her arms. "A little planetary argyle."

"I beg your pardon?"

"Just a concept I'm working on for a story."

"I thought you weren't working currently."

"I'm not. But I can't stop thinking of ideas for future articles. One of these days I'll be motivated to get back into writing mode. But for right now, I'm content to just ponder the possibilities."

"I'd like to hear about this 'planetary argyle' concept of yours," he chuckled. "But doesn't 'argyle' refer to a type of men's socks? The type that wives knit for their husbands?" He noticed her inquisitive gaze. "I'm certain that that's a memory I have with my own parents, actually," he added.

Amy looked at Cortland, at first bemused, but then he realized that she was studying him. "This is an interesting pause in our conversation," he said.

She didn't say anything, although she looked like she was about to. But from somewhere deep inside of himself, from that place where instinct subverts intention, he responded, "Maybe it's something I could introduce to the government."

And just as quickly she said, "Maybe it is."

"Would you like to have dinner with me tonight?"

"I'd like to go swimming right now. Care to race me to the water?"

"You're on." He gallantly let her run ahead of him, which of course afforded him the chance to watch her bikinied body run with a sensual grace that churned his legs to catch up to her as fast as they could, and he pulled her into the water with him. They splashed around like two kids for awhile, giggling and dunking each other until they inevitably gasped for air at the same time with their faces as close as two faces could be that weren't yet kissing each other.

And so he kissed her, first just a brush of their lips. And when they stopped and realized who they were each kissing, he saw that her breasts were heaving and her eyes looked hungry. His groin felt like it was boiling the water around them. He had to touch her breasts, so he put his hands on her shoulders and pulled them both into the ocean so that only their heads were in the air.

They stood like statues in the water that way, just staring at each other, each afraid to make a move that they knew would change their lives. He put her hands on his hips and moved his hands slowly up her belly until his palm and fingers held her breasts captive. At first he didn't move his hands, he just let them rest there, because he was aware that they were not alone. But he heard her groan, and he felt her nipples swell and change shape, hardening, pushing against his hand, trying to punch holes in her bathing suit.

He moved his hands away from her breasts and down her arms and he saw that her eyes looked cloudy. So he moved his fingers under the edge of her bra, slowly massaging her warm soft skin until he felt her nipples. He pulled them both under the water so that he could take each nipple into his mouth for at least a moment. They came up for air and his hands slid easily around her greased body until they landed on her hips and moved her towards him so that he could feel her on him, pushing on him, and still, they just looked at each other. And he couldn't help it but slowly, so only they would know, he moved her hips into his throbbing groin again and again.

They knew that they had done enough, but he took her head in his hands and moved her mouth into his mouth and they kissed, ever so gently, ever so slowly, and their bodies did the same. He felt her hand move lovingly over his penis, slowly and determinedly stroking it and exploring all of its parts, until she took the rigid rod into her hand and, understanding that it was imprisoned, rubbed it firmly and, with her other hand under his over-shorts, greeted its head as it pushed out of his bathing suit, and tenderly massaged it.

And as they still kissed, short, sensual kisses that they knew would be okay for the people on the beach to see, he moved his hand under the fabric of her bathing panties so that he could feel her hairs there, her lips there, her clit hardening under the pressure of his exploring fingers. He slowly put two fingers near her hole, and he wasn't going to, not here at the beach, but he slid them in, just a little, and he saw in her eyes how it felt so he stayed there a little longer. He touched her breasts again with his other hand.

They kissed, and held each other, and then they pulled each other under the water so that no one would see their bodies' spasms or hear their screams. His body exploded at the memory, and within minutes he was sound asleep.

REGA

The black limousine, with its darkened
windows, turned slowly off the heavily foliaged
suburban road where the trees were as tall as the Arc
De Triomphe, and the leaves and branches formed a
lush umbrella. Just before he made the turn, the
driver punched a code into the processor that was
built into the dashboard, and great iron gates opened
as the car approached them. The speed with which
the gates could be opened depended only on which
button was pushed.

Unless you knew that they were there, the
two rifled guards, one on the ground and one on the
columns that hyphenated the gates, were
imperceptible. As were the killer dogs that lurked in
the shadows.

The bulletproof stretch Cadillac wove its way
down the long driveway of the passenger's estate.
Caraway, he called it, named for his wife Caranina.
Caraway was a fortress, an armed camp, the rigor
mortised phallus of a man whose soul had been
replaced by an obsessive myopic revenge.

The passenger had thick black hair, enormous
dark brown eyes and large lips that would have given
him a lasciviously sexy look were it not for the
maniacal scowl lines of hatred that marred his olive

skinned face. As he was driven into his estate he thought, as he always did at this moment, that he would soon get his revenge and then he'd have even more riches than this.

As he walked up the three steps that lead to the mansion's entry, the steel encased mahogany doors were opened by a football player sized uniformed steward.

"Mr. Rega, sir. Lenny's got some messages for you. He's in the den."

"Where's my wife?"

"She's upstairs, sir."

"Tell Lenny to wait."

"Right, sir," the oversized overzealous manservant said as he took Rega's coat.

"You're learning, kid. You're gonna be all right. Just stop being so nervous every time you see me, okay?"

"Ah, yes, sir. Sorry sir, it's just that I really want to..."

"I said don't worry about it. You're doin fine, just fine. Now go tell Lenny I'll see him soon. And make sure we're all gonna have some dinner in a little while. Got it all now, Pepper?"

"Got it. Thanks, Mr. Rega. But...um..."

"What kid? What are you trying to tell me now?"

"My name's Paul, sir. Not Pepper."

"Oh, yeah. But I'm calling you Pepper. Okay with you?"

"Sure. Yeah. I like that. Call me whatever you want. Yes sir."

Another big strong kid that I don't have to pay much cause he owes me his life and he'll do anything I want him to do, Robert Rega thought as he climbed the gracefully curved staircase.

When he walked into their bedroom, Caranina was sitting in front of her dressing table brushing her strawberry tinted chin length wavy hair. She was aging, he thought, but she's still not so bad. And anyway she's stuck by me, and she pretends that she don't know that I fool around every once and awhile. That's a good woman. I'm a lucky man. It's a good thing that she don't know everything that's been going on. Otherwise she'd be outa here and don't I know that.

"We're having barbecue tonight, Robert. It's your favorite." She talked to him while she watched him in the mirror, and she saw him force a smile. "I'll tell you the truth, Robert. I had them make that as a bribe. So we'll go out to dinner one of these nights. I'm getting real sick and tired of having dinner here with your...," she paused to watch his face, "your new friends." Then she slowly spun around on her deep red velvet boudoir chair, which fabric matched the bedspread and curtains, and also the sofa that was in the alcove.

"You've been great, babe. You've been real understanding of my business pressures. But Robert never lets you down now, does he? You get all the dresses and goodies you ever want now, isn't that right?"

He understood that she had stopped calling him Rega, like everybody else did, years ago, after he started to make some money. She wanted to be all-American, like the other rich people that she saw when she went shopping. She married the wrong guy for that, he knew, although things started off right enough. She only talked about changing the last name once, he remembered, but he had convinced her that he was too well known in the business world to do that. She didn't know exactly how or why his world had changed, but she knew that it had, and he was trying to turn things around in the only way he knew how.

"Sure, Robert. I got everything. You made us a good life." She turned back to the mirror and said, "I'll meet you downstairs soon, okay? I still have a few, you know, female things to do."

"Sure. Just give me a kiss right here first, my pretty Caranina. Right here." He pointed to his cheek, leaned down to her mouth, brushed his cheek against her lips and stood up again. When he got to the door he told her, "We'll go out tomorrow night,

Caran. I promise." He'd been none too attentive to her for months, and he knew it. He had to keep her happy. He loved her, but he also needed her as an ally. And maybe for some other things too.

Rega went to his dressing room down the hall that adjoined the bedroom he often used when he stayed up late to formulate his plans, and when he couldn't sleep. He took off his suit, took a quick shower, and put on a pair of black silk slacks with a black cashmere vee necked sweater and went downstairs to the den to meet with Lenny.

"Hey man. You're looking real good Mr. Rega."

"Yeah I know, Lenny. What's up?"

"Well your old friend Heywood has called in some kind of special troops. So now we got some very mean men after you, you know?"

"Yeah? How mean? And what's so important or surprising about it that you have to come all the way here to tell me this?"

"Cause they're not only really mean. They're really smart."

"So what? That shit swindled me out of millions and my respectful life. But he doesn't think I'm smart enough to realize that he did that to me. And they're not smart enough to know it's me they're looking for."

"How long do you think it's gonna take for him to guess?"

"When it's too late, my friend. When it's too late."

MUSIC

The music was so loud I could hardly hear his voice anymore. What was he saying, maybe I'll never know, I thought. But then I clearly heard the beat. Boom boom boom, dah dah. Boom boom boom, dah dah. Wow. That's so sexy. What do I do now. Could you please make that a little louder. Is that the radio or a CD, I wondered. Oh, who cares. Just let me hear that music. It's so seductive, you know, it seduces me, I seduce you, you want to seduce me but I already seduced you so now look at you lying there don't you wish we hadn't been listening to that song.

"What did you say?" I said.

"Uh um um..."

"Okay okay. I'll let you hear the music too." So I took the tape off his ears and then, in a gesture of absolute selflessness and generosity on my part, I pulled off the duck tape from his mouth. I guess he hadn't shaved lately, I hadn't noticed soon enough, so he yelped a lot, but I knew nobody could hear him except me so I didn't really care. Asbestos soundproofing is a miracle. A miracle I tell you.

I was wondering should I do a wash, or just let everything stay so dirty and smelly. Oh, who cares, I realized. Who really cares. Some things get so dirty they can never be clean enough again.

46

I meant to pick up a quart of milk today and I forgot. I bought a whole cooked chicken instead and ate almost the whole thing. Where is my center, god damn it. Where is my middle eye, my soul, the white light, the neon sign. How the hell are you supposed to know which way to go. Doesn't anybody tell you, you're just supposed to figure it out for yourself. Look for signs, someone said. So, okay. Go this way, it said, but I went the other way instead, I always go the other way instead. Ironically, I am virtually bulletproof.

I have to pay attention, really concentrate so I do everything right from now on. From now on I'm gonna hone my craft. All of my crafts.

Now, what was I doing. Oh, yes, how I do veer occasionally and it's usually hard to get back on track. But when it's facing you right in your face, well, there you are and there it is.

There was this blond hair in front of me on a head with beautiful green eyes and blond eyelashes. How do I do it, I want to know. I'm so successful every single time. It's a miracle, I keep saying, I just can't help but admire the wonder of it. It was like spring today in the middle of winter, and he's wearing shorts and a running shirt. Well, that's how we met in Central Park.

He had been running with his cool blue and white sneakers, white with blue stripe socks, and electric blue shorts, with a white stripe down each side, and a white tight undershirt kind of top that was definitely not cotton and it clung to him and it was wet down the middle when he stopped after his run to catch his breath.

That's when he had caught my eye, when he leaned onto the wooden fence, bent his head down, sweat dripping from him, breathing really hard, his blond hair stuck to his forehead, the yellow little circular hairs on his arms all wet and shimmering.

I had been about twelve feet away, sitting on a park bench, looking adoringly at him how could he not notice. I was wearing all black, so surely I was as seductive as if he had met me in a dark club downtown at three in the morning. But we were in the park, and it was only two in the afternoon. We had the whole day and night to look forward to together.

"Hi," I said. What else can you really say at first anyway, I always wanted to know. You can't say things like 'have you been to the South of France.' That can't be the very first thing you say. There were only so many first things to say. You could say 'nice outfit.' You could say 'nice haircut, where'd you have it done?' You could say, 'great sneakers, what brand are they?' Or 'great watch,' 'great headband.' Stuff like that. Or you could do the weather. 'Really nice day, isn't it. What a gentle winter this has been.'

So then I said, "It's so warm, even though it's November. I wouldn't mind getting an ice cream cone. You look like you could use one too. Want to get ice cream together?"

He said, "Sure."

I said, "Great. Let's go."

He reached behind and pulled a thin piece of beige cloth from his back pocket, one of those fabrics that holds a lot more moisture than it should. He used it to wipe his brow. "My name is Roger," he said. "What's yours?"

"Rita. My name is Rita." I had my hair pulled back into a loose ponytail with a pink pearl strand dangling from it. I like pink with black. And I wore bubblegum pink lipstick, kinda like they wore in the 50's. Nice, really nice. Almost made your lips blend into your face but with a nice blush to them.

Anyway, so then he said, "Do you come to the park often?" and I said, "At least once a month."

Then he asked me, "Do you live in the city?"

And I said, "I have a home in the city and a home in the suburbs." You just don't want anyone to know too much about you right away, so better to be a little vague and mysterious.

"Where do you live?" I asked.

"Here in the city. All week long. All year long. Except I go to the Hamptons every summer. Do you?"

"Oh of course. The Hamptons, Bedford, Rhinebeck. Wherever there are little antique stores, summer houses and water, that's where you'll find me during the summers."

We giggled knowingly with each other, that we could be so cerebrally elitist, and so we walked a few blocks and got ice cream cones and kept chatting away. He was mesmerized by me, I could tell. When I asked, innocently of course, about his apartment, like what style decor he has, it was a nice conversation. So after awhile when I ask to actually see his apartment, maybe have a cup of coffee, I knew he'd say yes. They all say yes. The boys are so easy. If they think certain things are going to happen, they'll say yes to almost anything you ask them to do. That's just how they are. So very subtly I let them think that maybe they're in for a treat, and so then there is always this excitement in the air. It's great. And I was a bit smitten by him too, otherwise he would not have been the lucky one to spend all this time with me.

And this is how innocently it started. This is how innocently they all start. And just a few hours later, I'm a wreck, he's bleeding and blubbering, and I'm bored of him. I know everything I'll ever want to know about him and everything that is and ever was meaningful to him. I just want to leave and go somewhere else. Why do they all think I want to know so much about them? Why do they think I could possibly care so much? There comes a time when I just want them to stop talking please, thank you very much.

GRETA AND CORTLAND

"Cortland's a chameleon. He can look the look and talk the talk in any situation with any kind of people. I could put him in the trenches with the dirtiest fighters or in a tuxedo with kings and queens." Mr. G sat behind his magnificent mahogany desk, smoking a Monte Cristo No. 2 cigar, wondering why he felt the need to defend his most fiercely impassioned agent.

"You don't have to defend him to me, Garrison," Terence said. "I know that he is the consummate agent, and it's no secret that you have favored him."

"His talents made him worthy of that respect and recognition."

"I'm not arguing his extraordinary abilities."

"Then what are you saying, Terence. Could it be that you are envious of him?"

"Of course not, old friend. You know better than that." Terence looked at his colleague with concern, like a young man noticing his grandfather's impending fragility for the first time. "I've never heard you speak like this, Mr. G. I've never heard you not sound totally in control, all knowing and confident."

"Look. You're the only one I've told about

50

the take-over attempt. So I admit, I'm looking over my shoulders."

"But why to me?"

"To anyone. Of course it's not directed at you. But after thirty-five years of running this show, I'm absolutely not used to being challenged. That's all." But that wasn't all. As far as Mr. G was concerned, everyone was suspect. That was, after all, at least how he had made certain that his men were trained. He knew that was the only way.

When Garrison started GRETA, he was one of the wealthiest men in the world. At the time he founded and merged corporations that flowed billions of dollars into every world power and developing nation that he felt worthy. He was dear friend and advisor to every U.S. president in his adult lifetime. None ever suspected that he was running his own international intelligence operation.

Garrison's philanthropy was well known. But only he knew the reasons why he had been obsessed to create GRETA as a watchdog operation that would be secretly in existence as the self-appointed guardian of democracy. He started it not for political reasons, but, as far as he was concerned, for the most altruistic reason possible. He loved his country, felt indebted to it, and wanted to protect its integrity for purely benevolent, non-political reasons. So that it would remain the best, richest, strongest, wisest country in the world.

But now he was getting old, and someone was vying to take his place. He was fearful that GRETA, his life's work, would become as political as the partisan situations it originally sought to watch over.

AMY SAT

Amy sat in several days worth of her own excrement, which by this time was very little because they did not feed her or give her water very often and, when they did, the quantities were little more than subsistence level.

Always once, but sometimes twice a day, three men would come into her room, or take her into a special room, and question her about Cortland. They wanted to know what organization he was with, who gave him his orders, where he had been trained, and the names of other people who worked with him. She knew that Cortland was better off not having confided in her, and she was sure that her lack of knowledge was one thing that was keeping them from killing her. She had watched enough television and read enough books to know that it was only a matter of time before they would administer something like sodium pentothal to make sure they had really gotten all the information from her that she had.

After their interrogations they'd leave her alone, at least for a while, in what she considered her cell. She guessed that they had stripped a once charmingly furnished room bare so that she could never feel comfortable, so that she would want to tell them the truth and they would release her, as they kept promising they would. She slept on a two-inch mattress on the floor. There was a bathroom adjoining the room, but they sometimes kept the door locked. The only thing that comforted her was the pink and violet floral design on the partially ripped dirty wallpaper.

She had lost track of how many days they had kept her like this, as they had, after the second day, painted the windows black and then covered them with metal plates. Her best barometer of time was the degree to which her stomach aches increased, and how wet and smelly her torn and soiled clothing had become. She measured that today she would be rewarded with a shower, clean clothes and a decent meal. As heartening as that thought was, she knew that they only tended to her on a day that they were going to use her body.

She understood that her rapes were considered treats and entertainment for the men who were forced to guard her around the clock. They considered themselves as inconvenienced and imprisoned as she. Except that their stipend included fucking her, sharing their carnal good fortune with their visiting thug cohorts, and using her flesh to repay favors with people that were important to their world.

These men had repeatedly defiled the precious soul and exquisite body of an incredibly beautiful woman. Not one of them had ever met a woman of her caliber, or had seen a body as perfectly proportioned as hers, except in pictures in men's magazines.

From the moment this ordeal had begun, she knew only that she had to keep her sanity and she did so using various forms of mental and emotional calisthenics. In her mind she would follow every brush stroke of Cezanne's "Les Fleurs," and other paintings that she had long admired. Then she would recite, as poetry, every word to every song she could think of whose title started with the letter A. Then she would do the B's, C's, and so on. She could most engage her mind, however, when she created crossword puzzles with a minimum of twenty items both down and across which, because she was given no pen and paper, she had to memorize as she assembled them in her mind.

And when she felt that her thinking was lucid enough, she would try to think of ways to escape. But that was difficult, because she had no idea where she was. They had brought her here drugged and blindfolded, after first covering her face with a cloth soaked with ether. She didn't know if she had arrived by plane or car. She had begun, though, to piece together several theories based on the way the men who fed her and raped her dressed, spoke and behaved.

Their accents were New York street, and so were their clothes. And they were mostly the kind of men who had a macho dominance pathology. As long as she was in their midst, they needed to prove what they considered their manhood to themselves or to their friends, who would sometimes watch. As they raped her, she made a mental game out of how many of them approached her with worship, and how many played the role of her master and supreme conqueror. Occasionally they would send her a real romantic who thought their encounter would actually mean something good and special to her.

This morning she heard scraps of news, something about a new television program, something about a meal, something about a war somewhere. She remembered hitting her head against the wall till it bled and then she made daisy chains from threads of cotton she pulled from the ends of the sheet. She was proud of herself, she always was resourceful.

Thoughts of Cortland came often, and except for an occasional moving scrapbook of her early life with her family that played in her brain, those were the worst moments of all. Then again, if she hadn't made herself review the survival stories that he had unintentionally, but thankfully, instilled in her, she would have lost her mind on the first day of her kidnapping. They were supposed to let her go outside blindfolded for air for an hour or so a day with supervision. Sometimes they did.

She was trying to think of a five-letter word that started with an 'r' and ended with a 't' when she heard the keys jangling outside of her door. She smelled the food before she saw who was carrying the tray.

"I guess you must be hungry," said the shy young man of about twenty-five years of age whose eyes avoided her as he carried the tray of food. She had seen this boy only once before when he had come into her room with another man. Tory, as he had been referred to, had been given the task that first day of cleaning her room while she ate. He had carried with him a bucket of ammonia and a mop, and had been noticeably embarrassed that he was spreading around a nauseating chemical smell while she had ravenously consumed the food on her paper plate.

The man that had brought Tory into her room that first time had stood and watched her eat. He was Eddie, one of the men who had interrogated her with his squinty black eyes, oily black hair and a belly that looked like it had been stretched by too much beer and pasta and who reminded her of a nervous greasy drug dealer she had once seen in a movie.

When she had finished eating, Eddie had told Tory to get the other bucket and the shopping bag that he had left just outside her door. Tory had put the new bucket next to where Eddie was standing and watched as she was ordered to stand away from the mattress. Eddie had then ordered Tory to take the dirty sheets off the mattress, and replace them with the clean sheets that were in the shopping bag. When that was done, Eddie had told her to take off her clothes so that he could give her a washing down, as he called it, which is what he and his friends did with their cars, he had explained.

As loathsome as the thought was of taking off her clothes in front of these men, she had that day made the prospect of cleanliness more important than the revulsion she had felt. And although she had lowered her eyes to the ground as he wiped her body with the soapy sponge, she had looked up for a moment and saw that Tory's face was flushed and blushing. Still she had wanted to feel cleaner than this man was making her feel, so she had asked for the sponge and dipped it into the water and washed her body herself. And without asking permission, she had dunked her head in the bucket so that she could soak her hair and scalp. When she was finished, Eddie had told Tory to leave and he forced himself on her as she had suspected he would. When he left, she cleaned herself with her gray tee shirt and then put it back on with the old navy sweat pants they had given her.

On this day, Tory was alone with her and he watched as tears rolled down her face as she ate the biggest and most decent meal she had been given in days: baked chicken, mashed potatoes, spinach and a glass of milk. When she was finished he looked at her, his face red and sweating. He suddenly stammered softly, "they told me to do you when you finished eating."

She didn't let him see her disgust and instead looked him straight in the eyes and said, "But you don't really want to." Sensing that perhaps in this young man she had found the key to her escape, she continued, "You don't really feel that it's right, what they're doing to me, do you?"

"I, uh...I can't talk to you like that, you know," he whispered. "They'll get me if they find out. I'm just, uh, I'm just a worker here, in training, you know, with my uncle."

She didn't ask him what he was being trained for. "Well, they don't have to know if we don't really do it," she said, hoping she could better use the time to at least begin to talk him into helping her.

He looked over his shoulder to make sure that nobody was coming into the room, but he couldn't be sure that no one was listening from just outside the door. So he bent down as if to pick up her food tray and said, "I don't want to do it with you cause it's not right. But I want to do it with you more than anything in the world."

He was the only one, of the perhaps two dozen men she had encountered here, that showed any real sensitivity to her situation. She knew that she had to take a gamble with him. It was her only hope.

She took a deep breath and watched his face as she said, "maybe we can help each other."

"What do you mean?" he said as he put the tray down a few feet from the mattress.

"I've told them everything I know. I really honestly don't know any more. And I want to go home." She started to weep quietly, and the tears came easily. He looked at her with obvious pity and distress, but then he cleared his throat. "What do you mean help you. I can't help you. They'd kill me."

She looked at him imploringly and said, "Please. I know that you're the only person in the world who can help me. Please. I beg you. Please help me."

"Look. Stop crying, will you." And then with a bravado that she didn't think he was capable of, he said, "Listen to me. I'm gonna take off your clothes. And you gotta just stop crying and talking, and uh...see, I'm just another guy here and you have to do what I tell you to do. That's all. That's all lady."

He pulled off her tee shirt and sweat pants and just stared at her. "They would have killed you already if you weren't so beautiful, you know," he said as he pulled off his pants and said, "touch it. Touch it now." When she didn't move, he pulled her hand to him, opening her fingers and curling them around his distended penis.

The only thing she could think of saying was, "if I knew you would help me, I could make this really nice for us," she said as he kept his hand over hers so that he could force her fingers to press on him and rub him.

"No," he said hoarsely as he spread her legs and played with her breasts as if he was molding clay. Then he took his penis in one hand and tried to push it into her. But she closed her legs so that he couldn't, and he said, "oh I know what you want."

And when he moved his head towards her to kiss her, she turned her cheek to him.

"Don't you want me to kiss you?" She didn't answer him, stiffened her whole body, and kept her head facing away from him.

"Well then, fuck you," he said and spread her legs apart and violently pushed himself into her and came immediately while she lay there like a stone.

SAMANTHA

She was standing alone on the veranda wearing a wide brimmed black felt Coty girl hat with a brown and gray feather sitting diagonally on the charcoal ribbon encircling its crown. Her jet black hair skimmed the shoulders of the innocently suggestive black illusion sleeves that floated from the Mandarin collared blouse. Her black chiffon skirt fluttered rhythmically in the gentle breeze, harmonizing with the motion of the undulating ocean waves that seemed to have mesmerized her.

He had been walking with a purposeful pace until he saw her. His first thought was where are the cameras following this glamorous movie star, standing there posed for her fans to devour from the covers of magazines.

She turned around and saw him watching her, and in that instant he was jolted back to reality. She was far more beautiful than every picture and home movie he had seen of her. He continued to stare just long enough to see her long dark lashes blink and then aim her towards the sliding doors that would take her back into the Regency clubhouse.

He followed Douglas Heywood's daughter, at a distance, into the garden room and through the white marble hallway that led to the bar which was in an elaborately decorated room encased in pale coral marble walls and dimly lit by an enormous crystal chandelier. When he reached the room he could see her standing just inside its entrance, her back to him, as if she were looking for someone inside. When his left foot reached the threshold, she calmly turned around and said, "Cortland," as if it had taken her the long walk through the clubhouse to accept that it was him, the man who was going to explain why she might be kidnapped and killed at any moment. As if putting off the conversation would change the situation.

He only nodded, first because her astonishing beauty prevented him from uttering a word, and then because there didn't seem a reason to say anything immediately. She accepted the nod and his silence, turned and led him to a private table in a dark corner.

"Thank you for agreeing to meet me here. It's one of the only places father has let me visit. Otherwise I'm almost completely confined to the house." She knew there were protective agents discretely watching over her.

"I understand."

She spoke softly, not wanting to risk anyone hearing her. "There are guards surrounding the house. They even watch us eat through the windows." She looked at him, and he knew that it was taking all of her strength to hold back her tears. "All this is terrible. I feel so very childish complaining. The worst pressure is on father, of course. It has been unbearable for him."

"Your father is an exceedingly bright, very strong and courageous man. He has been living with threats for his entire adult life. He can handle this."

"I was told that you are one of the most capable intelligence men in the country. That you could probably single handedly make this all go away."

She had unintentionally broken the ice. Cortland reluctantly smiled. "I don't know where you got your information, Samantha. I would be happy to accept such a compliment from you, but that's not possible. Resolving anything of this magnitude is not possible to do alone. I appreciate your trust. You are endearing. Like a little girl, you would like there to be that one knight on a white horse who can wave a magic wand and make all of the bad things go away. Life isn't like that, you know."

"I've lead a very sheltered life. Actually, I've never had to deal with any hardships of any kind ever. This is the first time that I have ever felt traumatized. You must tell me what I should do."

"You must do as your father told you. You have to stay home and live surrounded by guards. You must also reassure your father that you are willing to do that. You are very precious to him. Your strength will help him feel more confident through this. Actually, I'm surprised that he let you come here today. I had assumed that we were going to meet at the house. Why did he let you out of the house?"

She looked at the napkin that she had been nervously rolling and ripping in her fingers. She was about to answer him when the waiter approached the table and took their order: two apple juices, no ice, and a platter of assorted finger sandwiches.

"It was my fault. I acted like the spoiled child that I am and had a mini tantrum. You have to understand, Mr. Cortland, that I've just spent the last months roaming free around Paris, and all of Europe. That was the first time in my life that I have ever been far away from home and on my own. To go from that to this claustrophobia got to me. I should not have carried on the way I did."

He thought she was finished speaking, and he was trying to decide if his response should be that of a stern teacher or a friend when she said, "We're surrounded by guards now, you know."

"More than you think."

"What do you mean?"

"Both your father's men and my men are here. But I still don't like the idea of your being out of the house. It's too soon. Frankly, it's too risky."

"Why?" She looked at him with her wide almond eyes, and he knew that she was hoping that she would find holes in his reasoning.

"When you are out of a controlled environment, like your home is right now, there are too many unknowns. There are too many possibilities for uninvited uninvestigated company. We can't search the members of this club without due process. We don't yet have any idea who is threatening your father. So at this point, it could be anyone. Even the bartender. If it is somebody your father knows, and who knows your family's habits, they could have joined this club to be able to get near him. Or you."

"I'm sorry."

RITA AND JASON

"Bet you're sorry you ever met me, aren't you I know you think you're so cute. Well, you're much cuter now that I put a few pretty pictures on you." She admired the stars and raindrops and flowers she had carved into his chest. "If you could only see what I see, how great you look now."

But all he said was, "Please. Please, help me. Please." The word 'help' came out sounding like 'hep' and 'please' sounded like 'pes' because he didn't have his tongue quite all in one piece anymore, so mostly he was making sounds.

"Look stop that. I have responsibilities to some people so I really don't have time to help you. But I'd like to kiss you goodbye now." She bent over to kiss his lips and there they were, all red and puffy like the fighters get.

She wore her black tights and long sleeve black tee shirt, black socks, black sneakers, hair in a pony tail, no make-up except for a little plum rouge. She knew she was pretty, but when she did these sessions with her night 'finds,' she wanted to be as neuter and neutral as possible. So no one would recognize her. But who could they tell, anyway.

Did they think it hurt them more than it hurt her? Didn't they know that she was in pain all of the

63

time, much more than the pain they felt right now. She wasn't belittling how much all of this must hurt them, of course, but they had to understand that theirs would only last for a little while and hers lasted all day every day of her life.

"Oh," she forgot his name. "Jason? Jason, is that you?"

He looked at her with his glassy eyes that were shiny with tears. He just stared straight ahead. She pushed him on his shoulder. "Jason. Answer me, Jason."

"Ummm. Uh."

"What are you trying to say, just say it right, will you?"

"Dhesa. Dhesa." He was trying so hard to agree with her, he didn't want to be hit anymore it all hurt too much. "Ehhhh."

"See, I was right I knew you were Jason. I like that name. Do you know what my name is?"

He didn't answer, so she shoved his shoulder again, not as gently as she did before, he didn't seem to appreciate how far she had traveled to spend all this time with him. She had to leave soon. She had to get home before somebody wondered where she was. She drank one more cup of the expresso coffee she had made in his kitchen. She was so zingy from the excitement and the caffeine that if there was no water between New Jersey and New York, she would have walked all the way back to the City.

"My name is Rita" was found written in fuscia lipstick on an antique white linen pillowcase that had three initials embroidered on its scalloped edge.

AMY CLUE

"We finally have something, maybe the pointers we need."

Cortland started to gulp down the last of his coffee, as if that part of the discussion was over. Then he put the cup on the table, looked at Brenner and said, "tell me."

"They found her gold Cross pen, the one you gave her. And a few inches from that they found a crumpled piece of paper."

"Okay, okay, what did she write on the paper?"

"She didn't write anything. But it was a piece of paper like from a hotel note pad. It said Mas D'Artigny."

"It said what?" Cortland's face reddened and his eyes became giant green orbs staring at his friend, frightening him. "That's where we stayed last year, in the south of France in the hills north of Nice." Then Cortland's face softened, and he smiled. "She either just dropped it, or she's telling us something."

"How could she have had the time, or the presence of mind?"

STOP IT

"Stop it stop it stop it. Oh oh oh no. No no. No more. Stop it please stop it it hurts. Oh please please stop. Stop." Just a few minutes ago he was crooning "Swanee River" to me. Now he's begging. God how to lose your sex appeal in my eyes in no time.

What was it an hour ago I said to him to stand there and sing to me. He was beautiful in his charcoal gray suit, black silk shirt, pewter and black tie, dark glasses, dark brown hair in a European way brushed back but not slickly and just skimming his shoulders. The only thing he wore that wasn't right were his black cowboy boots. The thing that was the most right was his voice. And the way his face and his body moved when his voice came out of him. I wanted us to be holding each other and dancing that Philly dance together with our bodies touching but then where would the music come from cause somehow I'd be making use of his mouth.

He thinks I love him but I don't. I just think he's so sexy. Oh I feel so warm and wet all over and when he stops singing I am going to take his hands in my hands and move my middle against his middle and just stand there and see what he does. And I think what he'll do is he'll move his middle towards me and

I will feel it right away, of course, and I won't be able to help moving right back towards him. Will we have a chance to smile or will we just start to kiss each other, with our soft lips and then our tongues all over the place. I can tell I won't know what to do first.

Oops now he stopped singing and now it's so quiet I really don't know what to do so should I get out that cute little carver with the U shaped blade, the one I used to carve the eustachian canals in my junior high school five senses carving of the inner ear, or should I just pull down his pants and suck on him for about half an hour. Maybe I could never make carvings on this one because I would always want him to be just a phone call away. I wanted to play with him right there in the nightclub but I couldn't I had to wait until we were in his apartment, on the couch, making out, moaning and groaning.

"I didn't know you had it in you," he said. I thought what the fuck are you talking about you can't imagine, even one percent, where I've been and what I've done. So now I'm mad. Now I don't care if I ever hear him singing ever again.

I don't care about anything, but this is the magic moment. This is my favorite part of it every time. That instant when I know what I'm about to do, but the guy thinks I'm still in lovey dovey mode with him. Sometimes I really believe it myself, cause, let's face it, this kissing and touching feels really good. But when the other mood hits, well, it just hits and that's about it. No one, except one, could turn the tide.

It's hard to pick just the right part of the wave of lust to make the move. The look and feel of surprise is priceless, it's something I've always wished I could share with someone. It's my very own warm mushy moment with my chosen ones.

We're kissing and touching, and moving and rocking, and hugging and laughing and he's looking at me with so much love and lust I almost hate to do it. But I have to do it. I just have to.

"So listen," I said to him. "What would you rather do. Make love to me or sing?"

He kept kissing and smooching. He couldn't believe I stopped to ask him a question he was so into what he thought we were doing.

I was getting annoyed. "Hey, come on. I really got to know."

"Right now I'd rather make love to you." And he went right back to kissing my neck.

So I kissed him back for a few minutes, so that he wouldn't suspect anything. Then he was kissing my lips again.

"You're so cute," I told him. "And you're even a better kisser than I thought you would be. I mean, I knew you'd be great, but you are incredible." So I let him kiss me some more. He really was turning me on. Sometimes when it gets like this I wonder if I should just keep going and get myself satisfied, or stop and get excited the other way. Either way I win. Wow, this is great. Maybe I'll just let him touch me a little bit, really get lost in me, then he'll be like a frog in formaldehyde, and he will have no idea what's happening.

I could tell he was working himself up to the moment and here it finally was, his hand starting to move down the front of my shirt. Slowly but surely.

So I let him. "Um ummmm," I said, and I really meant it. So then he got into a serious massage rhythm, first one breast, then the other. I still had my tee shirt on so big deal. Ok I'll let him do a little more, this was one of my favorite things on earth to do, who wouldn't admit that. First he rubbed one with his whole hand, sometimes touching the nipple and sometimes not. Ow. Sometimes circling the whole area, but always coming back to the nipple. Smart guy, this one. I was making noises, I sounded like a cat I once held, I couldn't help it so he just kept doing it more and more. He was still kissing me on my lips this whole time, and then I felt him move his hand away from my breast to my neck and just sort of play with my skin there for awhile. Oh, but I knew what he was going to do, and I have to admit I was happy about this. I could tell that he felt like he was being so cool and unpredictable, yeah right. But I liked the way he did it, he just moved his hand, fingertips first, into the vee of my shirt and wandered around for a little while as if he wasn't sure where he was going, yeah right. And then there he was, under my bra, heading for it, the nipple prize. Then he'll want to kiss it, probably, that's what always comes next, should I stop it now or let him keep going. I don't really mind all of this. And of course I haven't touched him yet I'm acting like such a spoiled princess.

I'm just kissing him back, actually. I'm saving my surprise for him for later. He's happy right now, rubbing his thing against me while he moves his fingers onto the actual skin. Around and around, then moving the fabric of the shirt away, then, for the first time he stops kissing my lips and slowly moves his mouth to my chin, my neck, down my chest and gives me these incredible wet kisses all over my boobs. Goddamn it this is incredible. Wouldn't it be something if we just kept going. Could he really make me feel that good.

Well, okay, even feeling good can get boring so I asked him, "What if you could never sing again. Would you just keep making love to me all day every day all of the time?"

He picked his head up for a second and said, "What? Did you say something?"

He's really into it now and I'm not so much in the moment anymore, as it were. I'm starting to think about other things. Like how I could get more enjoyment out of this little liaison that we're having. I mean, I'm a person too. I can't just provide the warm skin for him, what's in it for me.

So I ask him again, "What would you do if you could never sing again?"

"What, what," he says, and I can tell he could get exasperated pretty easily, "Do you want to talk now? Instead of being with me like this? Is that really what you want?"

He's clearly not used to a woman who is indifferent to his many charms and his prowess, and I don't want to disappoint him, but I've been through this so many times before it's enough already I can't really spend my time worrying about how he feels.

So I said, "Hey baby, listen to me. Forget what I was saying. Here's what. It's that I love everything you're doing to me. Now I have some ideas of my own. Some things I'd like to do to you. Can I play with you a little?"

I could tell by the look on his face that he thought that sounded like a really good idea. So I said, "Lie down on the couch, put your feet up, let me open your shirt, but you have to promise to close your eyes. Do you promise to close your eyes?"

"Yes. I promise. But I want to put a CD on first. What do you feel like hearing?"

"Put on your CD with you singing, that's what I want to hear, so I can remember what you sound like," I said.

He looked at me quizzically and said, "What?"

About an hour later, the CD was playing again for the third time.

CORTLAND SEES BLOOD

Cortland was sick to his stomach. "Listen, this isn't the worst I've seen, you know. But this is right up there. God what kind of tortured crazy creep could do this. Jesus! This is a monster, oh Jesus."

"Yeah I know, boss. I know," said Brenner. "But you'll get him, you always do."

They were both transfixed by the way the blood had clotted on the man's chest. In a background of dried red there were designs of dark red flowers and stems.

Cortland was wearing his trademark civilian outfit, a black raincoat with a navy, black and white plaid flannel lining. His style was almost fashionable, but never quite. He was handsome in a sandy way, with thick beige hair and caramel side burns. It was August so he was still tan, his green eyes looked very dark parenthesized by mushroom eyebrows that cascaded like two one-tiered waterfalls.

"What are these notes, 'My name is Rita?' I know the department has all the samples and they're in the cave already. Do you see anything here, Brenner? We have to know what this is. What the hell is this?"

"Calm down, Cortland. We'll have some

answers soon. I know what you're thinking. Look, I can't promise, you know I can't. But I'm praying with you, pal. I don't want this to have anything to do with the people who have Amy, either. No. The lab will know something soon. We just have to keep going and follow all the leads. And we will. Come on, Cortland. Let's get out of here and leave this to the chemists who can analyze the scene."

"I have to know who called this into the department. I have to know that as soon as possible."

"Just remember, so far the victims have been only men."

Cortland's knee jerk response, "That is, the victims that we've seen."

REGA TAPPING HIS FEET

Rega was tapping his feet, something he always did when he was getting impatient while he was sitting down. During his meeting with the boys he had finished a scotch on ice and was about to start another one when he realized that his wife hadn't sent the servants in yet, or her crazy assistant Belinda, to nag him about coming to the dinner table. He cared tonight because he needed her to do a few things for him, so he was ready to pay more attention to her than he had been but he couldn't do that if she wasn't there. This seemed like the way his plans were generally going lately, although he tried to keep acting tough in front of everyone.

So he checked himself in the mirror in the downstairs bathroom, straightened out his clothes and went upstairs. She was sitting where she was always sitting, in front of the mirror at her dressing table.

He walked over to her slowly, not with his usual domineering gate, the walk that he used to scare his men and keep them in line.

He went over to her and put his hands on her shoulders. She was shaking under her evening gown, her chosen attire for their dinners at home when there was company. This gown was a sleeveless pale yellow chiffon empire a-line that went to her ankles. She had bought it because it had a white crinoline slip under it and the whole thing swished when she walked.

Four hours earlier she had called all over the house looking for Belinda, and finally, two hours ago, her faithful Belinda spot cleaned the dress, purse and shoes. Yellow stained so easily.

"Caran. My pretty Caranina. Chill baby, do you know what I mean. I know you do, just relax and settle down. Why are you so nervous? Do I look that good to you that you just can't help yourself? I tried to look good for you tonight, you know."

She looked at him, from the top of his head to his toes and then her gaze settled on his eyes. "I know you dressed for me tonight." He was wearing the black velvet formal slipper loafer, with the gold and red crest embroidered on its toe, that she had bought for him at Hermes. Oh, she loved them. He had also put on the black and gray silk Gucci smoking jacket over the gray silk slacks. She wanted to touch him on his thigh, or on his chest, but she didn't. Her green eyes looked beautiful against her porcelain skin with her light red hair fluttering against her shoulders, with a few wispy bangs floating across her brow.

This whole thing is sick, she thought. Didn't he know it?

"Caran. I know you're mad at me. I know I haven't been paying a whole lot of attention to you in awhile. But please, baby. You know you're still my baby. I know I've been with the guys a lot. Okay, I've been with the guys too much. That's it with you, I know that's it. We haven't had a dinner alone together. We haven't gone out anywhere together alone. We haven't..."

Did he miss having sex with her, did he want to have sex with her now, or did he just want to act like he was interested. To keep her happy. When did it change. For years he had to have her. He used to ache all over for her he could hardly walk or think about anything else but the way she felt when his hands moved around all over her. Maybe it changed when she acted like she didn't care about him anymore, didn't move up against him in bed anymore. Even when he started with her, she didn't melt anymore. He knew he wasn't losing his charm, cause the other girls still did what he wanted them to. All ages. But he had to keep this one happy. She was who he actually loved, he didn't always realize that he was hurting her. Once she did realize and she almost did something foolish. Maybe that's when it changed. When she started doing things that were almost as crazy as some of the things he did.

WHY IS HE STILL HERE

"Why is Frank still hanging around here, I don't get it," Rega complained.

"What's the matter, why are you upset," Cara asked him.

"Cause wherever we go, whatever I'm trying to do, Frank keeps showing up. I gotta talk to him. I don't know what's going on with him. It's gotta be that he wants a better position with me, I don't know why else he would keep hanging around like this."

It was summer. People were going to the beach, it's lighter later, that always feels festive.

But Frank had called earlier to see him, so Rega decided to take a ride to the beach houses where Frank had a little place. I'll stop by there, Rega thought. See what he is trying to talk to me about.

So he did. He drove to the side of Frank's house, and noticed that for the summer it looked closed up already, curtains on most of the windows. Maybe he had to go away, and that's what he was trying to tell him. Then he saw him walking towards him.

"Hey Rega," Frank shouted. "What brings you here," he was stammering, looked kind of shot from something.

"Just taking a ride around, heard you called,

thought I would stop by. What's on your mind, Frank?" He paused, considering his next question, Frank looked really weird. "What's the matter Frank, you don't look so good."

"Well Mr. Rega, I'm having a little, I guess you could call it a little party inside." He looked down at his feet. Then he said, "That's why I called you. I did something special for you."

What could this be, wondered Rega. "What is it," he asked, "what do you mean you did something special for me." Whenever Frank does something extra, more than what he's told, it's a disaster.

"Well, remember that man you were trying to track down, that I was helping you with. You know, your government friend. But we had no luck."

"Well of course I remember that, Frank. Your help was great. One of these days maybe we'll actually find him. I'm still working on some possibilities." He watched Frank's face, he looked like he had a big announcement to make. "What it is?"

"Well, I went to your house to tell you, but sometimes you get so mad when I just show up. So I just did it, something special for you, I wanted to surprise you with it."

"What Frank, what. I know you're always trying to be helpful, I know that. It's just that sometimes things don't need helping."

"Well, remember when we were trying to find your government friend, remember who we found instead."

Rega thought about that for a minute, and remembered. They had finally tracked down where Heywood lived, and by then Rega was fed up with all the applause Heywood was getting from the whole goddamn world because of him. One day Frank saw a car go in and out of the grounds and he followed it, all the way to the beach. He watched the man who had visited Heywood pick up a girl. She was gorgeous. He watched when he took her home. He remembered her address.

"So, what are you telling me, Frank?" Rega was getting nervous, Frank was more unhinged than he was.

"We have her, she's here."

"You have who, who is here."

"We have the spook's girl, she's in the house, we're trying to get information from her for you. I did this for you Rega."

"You what the fuck?" Rega was crazed. "What do you mean you have that girl in the house?"

"Well don't you want to come in and have sex with her? She's having sex with everyone." Frank waited to see Rega get enthused about this, but he didn't. "She hasn't told us anything yet," Frank stammered. "I thought holding her for you would make her talk."

"What, do you think you're in a movie Frank? I really hope you're lying to me Frank. You better be fuckin lying to me. Because if you are not lying to me, you better set that girl free right now, right now. And I don't ever want to hear about this again. Cause you better be fuckin lying to me."

Rega was pacing and sweating.

"I gotta fuck her again. You should really come in here and get her before we let her go. She isn't telling us anything anyway."

"What are you out of your mind!" Rega screamed. "I didn't ask you to do this. I didn't tell you to do this. We are already causing enough trouble what the hell did you do now!" Rega was dripping with sweat.

"Stop trying to do me favors, Frank. This isn't a favor. Get her out now, put her someplace where she will be found, but don't get caught. Don't you dare get caught."

"But Rega, I did this for you, don't you see. This is getting you closer to finding your man. I'm always trying to do something special for you."

Rega drove away. The next day he read that a homeless woman was found on a bench at the Great Neck train station, the police took her in for questioning to try to identify her.

AMY FREE

Cortland drove through the streets of Stamford, Connecticut like a rubber band missile. Amy, at last. Oh God, please let her be all right. Or at least healable, he prayed to the dashboard as he changed the channel to the all news radio station.

She had been found dressed in gray sweat pants, sweatshirt and sneakers on the bench at the Long Island railroad station in Great Neck. As if she were about to board a commuter train. One of the off-duty conductors noticed that she never stood up to get on a train, she just sat there. He called the police. The security cameras showed her approaching the bench along with a mob of the regular rush hour travelers.

She told them that her name was Amy Killington. She screamed when they tried to touch her to lead her into a car. When she babbled on believably about government connections, they thought it best to contact Storch, a top security military and government psychiatric hospital that catered to the reconditioning and rehabilitation of assorted international leaders and operatives whose mental capacities had been compromised in one way or the other. This is also where hostages of note were taken to be debriefed and reentered into society.

And it was the first leg on many a life time journey for VIP's forced into the government's deepest cover protection program, when identities, physically, mentally and on paper, were altered. And there were those who were sent there for the sole purpose of being broken, disintegrated and diffused. They already had the name Amy' Killington in their system so she was admitted immediately.

In his phone call just hours ago, the institution's Director, Commander Cheshire, had told him to prepare himself for Amy to be in a very delicate post-traumatic state. He had said not to have unrealistic expectations of their first meeting, not to expect too much of anything for awhile. He had been purposefully vague on the phone, Cortland understood, but some substance had certainly been conveyed. How long is 'awhile,' Cortland asked. We really can't say, was the reply. He arranged for Cortland to meet with her doctor for a briefing prior to seeing her.

His visit had been arranged through top priority channels, so that when he arrived at the facility, the doctor and a guard were waiting for him.

"I'm Doctor Olden, Mr. Cortland." The two men shook hands, and without hesitating the doctor continued, "Please come to my office." When they arrived, the doctor nodded to the guard, who closed the door behind him as he left the two men alone and took up his post outside of the office.

After a few necessary formalities, the doctor began. "As you might have imagined, Miss Killington, Amy, has been interrogated, drugged and abused. Truthfully, I am amazed that a woman, who has had no professional training whatsoever, was able to survive and at least presumably keep her sanity in a very insane and brutal situation, and exhibit such an incredible will to live. You and I have both known many pros who have broken down after far less than she has endured."

"How bad, Dr. Olden?"

"I won't soft-pedal anything for you, Mr. Cortland. She's only just arrived, so she hasn't been through all of the tests and observations. She is holding on for dear life. It's like she's standing near the edge of a cliff, and she knows that if she takes one more step, she might never find her way back. That is, indeed, how close to the edge she is."

"I want to know everything that happened to her."

"Of course I will tell you everything I know, and as quickly as I can, for now."

"As much as I want to see her immediately, I would rather take whatever time is necessary to be fully informed before I see her, Dr. Olden."

"Under other conditions I would respect your wishes and your senior rank and classification, Mr. Cortland. But, I must be frank with you. The sooner you see her the better. Actually I'd say it's as nearly a matter of life and death as I've ever seen. In the short time that I've spent with her, it is absolutely my judgment that her thoughts of you are what kept her alive."

He paused, and then added, "Please be prepared, she has been deprived of proper nutrition, she has been treated badly physically. She is thin, she has bruises, she has not been able to shower or bathe. Understandably she does not want to be touched by strangers, so we had to give her a sedative to help clean her."

Cortland allowed himself a nano-second of emotion, and then commanded, "You will take me to her immediately and tell me as much as you can on our way."

The two men hurried through the halls of the hospital. "We assume her kidnappers drugged her with a darted shot that she could not possibly have seen coming, we were able to detect the hole in her skin where the dart hit," the doctor continued. The additional information relayed in their conversation was driving Cortland to further quicken his pace. He felt sick, he wanted to vomit, but he made Dr. Olden continue. As they approached the end of a long corridor, Dr. Olden slowed down. "We're here."

Cortland started to reach for the door handle,

but the doctor interrupted the movement. "I have to tell you one more thing. I'm not certain what she looked like before, but I must tell you that her appearance reflects what she has been through. She looks ravaged, undernourished, disoriented and frightened."

"I did this to her," Cortland said.

"I understand."

"I'd like to see her alone. Would that be all right?"

"Of course. Either I or a nurse will be outside of the door should you need anything."

"Like what?"

"She hasn't had one yet, but a seizure would not be that unusual. Her entire person is in shock. The shock waves can show themselves in many ways. She might lose control, and you might not feel capable of handling it. She may need to be subdued. There are so many possibilities. You know her well. And you're well trained. Follow your instincts."

Cortland inhaled deeply, then slowly measured three steady breaths as he focused his eyes on the floor. When he felt composed, he opened the door and walked in. As he closed the door behind him, he looked into the room and felt his feet turn into lead weights.

Amy was lying on her bed in a fetal position, eyes closed, every few seconds rocking her body to a rhythm only she heard. She seemed oblivious to her surroundings. She certainly did not seem to be aware that anyone had just walked into the room.

He walked quietly towards her and, when he was a few feet away from the bed he said, "Hello Amy," in as soft and gentle a voice as he could summon, which used, anyway, all the strength he had at that moment. She seemed not to have heard him. He tried again. "Hello, Amy. It's me, it's Cortland. I'm so happy to see you again. We were looking for you."

Her movement startled him. She sat up abruptly in her white and blue striped hospital gown, her hands turned into fists pushing down against the mattress, which gave way to her force like a marshmallow, her legs dangling lifelessly over the side of the bed. He was drawn to her eyes. In just a few moments they were cold, then panicked, then questioning. Then there was a glint of recognition. Then she was crying.

Cortland quickly sat beside her and began to put his arms around her. As soon as he touched her, she screamed. Loud piercing primal animal screams.

He forced his arms around her and cradled her like a baby. As he rocked her gently he said, "It's all right now, Amy. It really is me. It's Cortland. Nobody is going to hurt you." He continued to talk this way and rock her, and slowly her screams turned into deep wracking sobs that convulsed through her tormented being.

He sat with her like that for over an hour until he realized that she was drifting off to sleep. He moved her body onto the bed and covered her with the blanket.

He phoned the doctor from the nurse's station and explained what happened. Within moments the doctor ordered a sedative shot for her, to assure that she would sleep. He had no way of knowing that he was also quieting the voices.

RITA'S HEAD

She's always mourning one thing or another. This time it's the loss of blood. Last week she lost a ring that was given to her by Santa Clause when she was eight, her mother's friend who used to put on a white beard, mustache and red outfit, even when it was summer, before her mother came home from having lunch with the girls. He said he was her special husband and didn't she know that meant that they were married, her and hairy him, so she had to act like his wife. What did that mean did she have to cook for him and clean the whole house all by herself she had asked him. No, he had said, not things like that 'my pretty petunia,' which is what he always called her.

The first time he pulled down his pants and told her to look she was amazed. All she could think of was it reminded her of the big nose on an elephant, hanging there, swinging around, so she asked him how come he had a part hanging from him that was like what an elephant had.

She never told her mother. Her mother was always so shaky and scared about everything anyway.

After that he showed it to me whenever he thought it would be more than an hour before my mommy got home. Sometimes he told me to touch it. Once he asked me to kiss it goodnight. Mostly he told me to watch him pushing it against the arm of the couch like he was riding a horse like they do in the cowboy movies, a bucking bronco at the rodeo. Then he left me alone for a long time, I was glad to have time to go out and play with my friends again. Then I saw him with one of my friends and now I knew why she was always crying. So the next time he told me to pull his pants down and kiss it I grabbed it and hit it as hard as I could with my hairbrush. He was yelling at me when my mommy got home and she said what was going on, what was all the ruckus about.

Moms, she liked to be called because it made her feel like she was from the higher classes, she always expected so much from me I was her shining star. I can see why. I was adorable and so talented, and everybody liked me because I could be whatever I wanted to be that day, but I was so dizzy inside all of the time and I never told anyone. What could anyone do? I knew I was not all there about some things and really brilliant about some other things. Which one was most of the time was the hard thing to figure out.

Was I pretending to be that other person then, or was I pretending to be this person now. This was too much to ask. As long as I lived somewhere and could go shopping and then hide, all was okay enough. When I was a little girl I told him what was happening to me, I know he didn't believe me, but he promised that he would protect me.

I never stayed away too long, just long enough before anyone would think it was odd. When did people start watching me like that, maybe it was just my imagination and nobody ever missed me at all. I used to have my own apartment, I used to have so much, how did I lose it all and then I had to start all over again. Where did everything go? Who packed the dishes? Who took my boyfriend? Who took my life?

Would they find out who she was? Would she? Was it me?

AMY SLIPPING

Cortland was jolted from a nap by a phone call. He listened intently to what the doctor was saying, knowing that he was supposed to read the unspoken and the unthinkable between the lines. "I'm on my way," Cortland said numbly, nearly inaudibly, into the phone. Amy's equilibrium was slipping again, the doctor said. Part of her was trying desperately to hold on. Which meant that another part, Cortland deduced, could let go.

It was one o'clock in the afternoon when he arrived at the hospital. It was a warm and sunny summer day with the humidity, mercifully, at an unseasonably comfortable level. He wondered to himself why that mattered, and knew that the guilt he felt for Amy's kidnapping and instability was as mentally grating as the heat was suffocating. Nevertheless, when he pulled into the hospital's parking lot and heard breaks squeal, he realized that they were his.

Dr. Olden hadn't conveyed that Amy's condition was an emergency, but Cortland flashed his security badge to the guard and ran through the hospital's front door. He nearly bumped into a cart of medication as he sprinted towards the doctor's office.

"Cortland. I'm glad you were able to get here this fast."

"What's happening with her? Don't be as vague as you were on the phone."

"Follow me. I'll explain while we walk."

Dr. Olden explained that Amy's personality was not integrating well, and that at this juncture there might be cause for alarm. Her fits were becoming more bizarre and uncontrollable, and, worst of all, she had begun to hurt herself again.

"Frankly, it's as if we have to start at square one with her treatments," Dr. Olden said sadly. "For all of this time, she gave every sign that, no matter what it took, she intended to recover. Now she has clearly regressed, to a surprising, however not unusual, extent." He paused and looked at Cortland's face. "The spark of life that she had held on to seems to be slipping. We will continue to do everything we can for her, of course, but she must be at least somewhat willing to go through the psychological and physical therapies. You had to know."

"I'll work with her more, doctor," Cortland stammered. "I'll do..."

"You have taken on a tremendous burden, Cortland, and I understand all of the reasons why. It's true that you have been her primary source of hope. But judging from her recent state of mind, I'm not sure that even you can give her what she needs. I'm not sure if anyone can help her quite this soon. She needs more time."

"What are you saying?"

"It really comes down to this, Cortland." The doctor shifted his feet and looked away to steal a moment of mental seclusion, and so that Cortland couldn't see his eyes as he reviewed the horror that his patient had been submitted to. When he was ready to articulate his thoughts in their lowest common denominator he said, "The degree of intensity involved in her trauma is, at least, the degree of persistence that she must apply to her recovery, and therefore her very survival." He paused, then continued, "Look Cortland, she's been traumatized as much as any woman I've ever seen. I don't know how she survived. As a lay person, as a human being and as a doctor, I do not know how she survived that. But whatever she reached for inside of herself to do that, she just better have enough left to take her through this part."

"I'm not sure what you're trying to tell me. What do you think her prognosis is?"

"I know that, while it was happening, she had an extraordinary will to survive the torture she was subjected to by her captors. I'm not sure if she has the will to survive its aftermath."

Even though he was in an air-conditioned facility, sweat was dripping down Cortland's neck into his shirt. He looked at the doctor and said "I have to try."

"I know you do. Please, come back to my office before you leave the building."

Cortland went into Amy's room and was amazed to find her brushing her hair in front of the mirror. From what the doctor had said, he had expected her to be lying in bed and a mess. Perhaps, he thought hopefully, knowing he was on his way to see her had helped snap her out of a mood that the doctor had read into too deeply.

She was wearing an outfit that he had brought from her home a few weeks before, baby blue pants and sweater with matching leather moccasins. She looks so much like her old self, and he was as dazzled by her natural beauty as he had been the day they met. He smiled as he walked towards her and said, "Amy. Oh Amy. You look wonderful today."

After she saw his reflection in the mirror, she turned around slowly and said, in a voice that sounded eerily tortured but composed, "You know, of course, that I am two people now, Cortland. I'm Amy. Sure, I'm Amy. I know that I'm Amy." She reached slowly behind her to put her brush on the dressing table. She looked at the floor and continued, "It's true, of course, that I'm Amy. But, now, that's also a lie."

She looked at Cortland with glazed and sad eyes. Her faint voice had become a mournful dirge.

"As you can see, I can make myself look like Amy. I can even act like Amy. But really, I'm not Amy anymore. Amy's gone. I can remember things about her. How she looked, how she acted. That's how I know that sometimes I can pretend that I'm her. But I'm not her."

Cortland got on his knees in front of her and held both of her hands. "Amy. Listen to me. By god, after what you've been through, I don't know a human being who could just snap back into their old life or a new life. But the doctors here have seen many people through the hell you're feeling. And they can help you too. Dr. Olden told me that in just a little more time, you are going to be on your way to feeling fine, Amy. You just need to keep working with him. And with me."

With the same ghostly voice she said, "You're just saying that. To be kind. But you see, I know things that they and you can't know."

"Tell me, Amy. You know you can tell me anything."

Her body became rigid, her voice cold and far away. "You sound just like them. Everybody wants answers from me. That's all anyone wants. I told everyone that I don't have the answers that they want." Her body shuddered.

"Amy. I'm Cortland. I'm not one of those awful people who were hurting and interrogating you. Neither are any of the doctors. We all love you, Amy. We all care about you and want you to get better. Nobody wants to hurt you. All of that is over."

She stared through him. "I'm in a dark forest. I know there's sunlight up there somewhere, but I can't see it. And I'm not sure if I'll ever see it again. How do I get to it, Cortland? It's very dark and cold where I am."

"It'll just take a little more time, Amy. And then you will start to feel better. I know you will."

"You tell me you love me, that everyone here loves me. You used to love me. Now it's a different love. You don't understand, but I do. I'm not a real person anymore." She looked down, then looked into

Cortland's eyes. "I am not a real person anymore."

"Of course you're a real person. And I know that in just a few weeks you and I are going to go out for a wonderful dinner. There's a whole world out there Amy. I'm going to bring you back into it."

As if she hadn't heard him she continued, "I look at you, and I feel like I'm in a...a...a time warp. You haven't changed. You just feel so guilty. Hey, every relationship is a risk. Ours just had more unseen dangers than most. And so now it's as if I'm looking at you through field glasses. You're far away. And I can't get to you." She reached out and touched his face. "I see you there. I feel you. The warmth of your skin. The light in your eyes. I used to have a light like that in my eyes. But my lights went out."

"Please listen to me..."

But she didn't. She just kept talking. "I feel like I'm a stranger. To you. To myself. I can't get my bearings. I know that what I'm saying makes sense. But even my voice sounds far away from me. Like it's not coming from me."

He tried to sound positive, but he was pleading with her now. "Will you promise me that we can go out to dinner soon. That's all I want to know from you today. I want you to wear exactly what you're wearing now. We'll go to your favorite restaurant. You used to love L'Absynthe. A glass of red wine, their bread, their wonderful French food, the waiters. You loved it there, Amy. We'll talk and laugh just like we used to. Wouldn't you like that, Amy?"

She cried without tears, "I'll smile because you want me to, but my eyes won't smile. I'll laugh, but nothing's funny anymore."

And then suddenly she snapped out of her trance-like state and, for the first time since he walked into her room, she connected with him. Her eyes were clear, her thoughts seemed lucid. The muscles in her face relaxed, her voice sounded almost maternal, her words understood his tortured need. She smiled at him and said, "Yes. Yes we will do that Cortland. Yes, I want to do that more than anything else in the world."

And two weeks later they did, as they had tried once before, but that time was too soon. This time Amy was able to walk with a healthier stride. When she looked around at the other patrons she didn't wince, and she was able to look at the menu and make an easy choice. Cortland held her hand across the table. He didn't really care about eating. He was just so happy to have at least the semblance of a normal time with her. The doctor was being over cautious, he thought.

SHUT UP

"Shut the fuck up," I said. "Just shut up. I tell you to be quiet nicely and you don't listen so excuse me, but I have to say it harsher so you know I really mean it."

She stared at her friend lying there whimpering. "What is with you why can't you stop this. You liked everything I did to you. I know you did. So show your appreciation a little bit and just..."

She leaned in to her friend, turned him on his side so he faced her. He really grimaced then, and when the knife that was sticking out of his side rubbed against the bottom of the shelf that he was under he screamed.

"Shut the fuck up," she screamed, at first calmly, then on top of her lungs. "Shut the fuck up. Will you just shut shut the fuck fuck up your ass mister. I have had it now. If I thought we were finished then, I know I've really had enough of you now."

Then she heard him. "What...what did I do? Tell me what did I do?"

She couldn't believe it. Hadn't she cut his tongue out? She thought she did. She always did when they cried so much she couldn't take it. How could he keep talking like a goddamn snowball rolling down a long hill you just can't stop.

The evening had started off so nicely, she thought. I was sitting in the car, his car, in the passenger seat and I had the most incredible urge to unbutton my jacket so that he could see I was wearing a black lace tee shirt without anything under it. I didn't want him to see the whole thing right away, of course, just a hint of it so he'd realize how sexy I looked and he would get crazy and horny. This is just a platonic friend, I intend to keep it that way. A girl needs a platonic male friend. For appearances sake, at least. There are so many places one must go. Dinner parties, movies, someone to have sushi with when I don't have a date. He'd never believe me if I told him what I really am. He thinks I do research for a pharmaceutical company, just like I tell everyone I meet. And I sort of do, actually, a girl has to support herself.

He wondered why we didn't talk as much as we used to. That the phone number he had for me isn't really anywhere I ever am it's just a service.

"God damn it fuck this. Just up yours to you know where, where the sun doesn't fuckin shine, that's where." Why am I cursing like a drunkin sailor, I don't know why. Maybe I shouldn't have done this to him, he was my friend. Damn fuck shit. I wonder if I even know all of the curse words. I can retrieve them on command from my computer brain, I even know all the modern clichés. I told you I went to college.

Maybe it was just all a dream.

HI HONEY I'M HOME

I didn't have time to change. This is the first time this ever happened.

"Hi honey, I'm home." Every single day. Every single day. Over and over again. There certainly must be another way to say it but I'll be damned if he would ever think to think of it. What is wrong with people sometimes. Here he is again, climbing up the stairs. Is it always on the seventh step, of the twenty steps, that he starts. Although sometimes it's right away on the third step. Hi honey, I'm home.

Oiy. Malang. Bevo Caramia. What now my love. Was he at the top of the stairs yet. Should I stay here, or should I lie on the bed unsuspectingly. Or should I hide in the closet or in another room down the hall. What oh what should I do, little boy blue. Oh where oh where should I go, do you know. And most important, what should I wear.

Maybe they're all the same. And it's just a bunch of words, anyway. The indignities of it all. A little manslaughter followed by a dash of misdemeanor battery, a lindy with the prosecution, where's the proof, no multiple batteries in this flashlight. So let's make a deal, and garnish it with a pinch of immunity. Then you can play again. A felony conspiracy, a measure of revenge. And now I'm spring cleaning. Thank god I never lost my looks. Go figure.

What is going on for her, can she reinvent herself in this fish bowl full of guppies and sharks, tadpoles and uteri. Ta da dum dum da da!!

"Hi honey I'm home." If I loved him I'd show it. If he loved me he'd know it and show it and I don't know which one is an act. Eyewitness news can you hear me can you see me what's up. What's happenin man. Dis and dat. Whas dis, whas dat. I'm so nervous I'm babbling. I didn't have enough time. There wasn't enough time.

"What the hell kind of outfit is that, Caran. What the hell are you wearing. Shit you don't even look like you I don't know what the hell you look like," he said.

Think fast, think fast, yes, I can do that I can think fast. I'm the master of think fast.

So I didn't move, I just stood there, trying to look as much like Audrey Hepburn in *Sabrina* as someone who looks like me possibly could. I would much rather be eating a bowl of chocolate ice cream right now than going through this. Jesus this is tense.

"Hi dear," I sighed. "It's my new exercise outfit. I'm just trying to be modern for my Rega." I looked for belief in his face, in his eyes, but he just stood there staring at me. So I kept trying. "And I thought it would look sexy for you. Something a little different, huh?"

Rega was stunned. "Different. Yes, this is different." He only ever saw me in lovely pant suits and dresses. His Caran would never wear this. So I walked slowly to him, to try to prove that what I was saying was real.

Some days he smells of another woman. When he walked by me on his way to his shower, to wash her off, to put on his talc, put on his cologne. Whiff. I always knew. It was in the air, it was in his walk, it was in his eyes, his smirk that wasn't for me. It was left over from her.

He said, "Tell me again, Caran, what kind of

outfit is this. Your hair. You look like you're trying to be thirteen again, but my beautiful lovely Caran...this is not my Caran."

"Okay my darling, I'll change for you right now, and from now on I will change at the gym so that you will never have to see me in these outfits again."

AT THIS VERY MOMENT

And so I'm looking at you, and I'm thinking what did you think – what exactly did you think I would do right now at this very moment. There, you know how much I care, you're standing right there in front of me, you have tears in your eyes. And what – what are you trying to tell me, that you found somebody else, that it's not me who you love anymore?

Tell me, you gotta tell me, what did you think I would say at this exact moment. What did you think – did you think that I would stand here and start swearing at you, and say anything and everything that I can think of to hurt you – all because, now I know, now I know for sure, it's just not me who you love any more.

I bet that you thought that I would hate you after you told me, that maybe I'd hit you, what, you've always thought that you knew me so totally. I never thought that I could hurt you or anyone else, but especially you because I love you so much, but I don't know, hmmmm let me think about it but I still don't think I could ever hurt you.

But more than anything else in the world, I want to know what do you think I would want right now, if you'd only stay, then you know what, could you possibly even realize what, that I would change my life just for you, I would even go back in time. I would right now fall on my knees and I would beg you if baby, my baby, if I could just be with you and hold you again. I'd give anything. But since you just don't seem interested at this very moment, I'll have to deal with it in some other way.

I'll get down on my hands and knees all right, just to throw you off guard. I'll look like I'm about to kiss the ground that you walk and talk on, but then I actually change my mind and instead I take my twenty-inch knife and push it through the middle of you. Boy, you looked so surprised, then I asked you what song you wanted to listen to, and you looked like you were really trying to come up with an interesting request. But you never followed my rules, or met my expectations. Instead you kept surprising me, delightfully surprising me I should say, with really interesting takes on things, interesting life experiences, a soulful love of music, I thought you would think that you wished instead of this that we had been pen pals only always rather than ever actually meeting, but I caught you off guard.

AMY AND HER DOCTOR

She saw unimaginable things on television like a horror movie. She had silently marveled at the special effects. The buildings falling down. But it had really happened. She was shocked, she felt disconnected. Things in the world were not the same as they were when she left that day. She had been so happily riding her bicycle to the market.

She was wearing a gray flannel long sleeve, ankle length, loose housedress, with slip-on gray moccasins and gray socks. She looked like a refugee from somewhere. And in fact, she knew, she was a kind of refugee.

Now she felt a new kind of alert, realizing you can feel sorry for yourself until you realize that many people experience so much worse.

Woe be me no more. This feels like a story I wrote, she thought. I am so tired of having to prove myself. I just did. I survived that.

She picked up the phone installed in her room that she had never used. There was a voice asking what number she wanted to call. Except for the night out at the restaurant that Cortland navigated, it was the first voice from the outside world that she had to deal with on her own.

"I'll... I'll..." and she hung up. Okay, slow

down a little before you do anything, it's all right, she reassured herself, as if she were calming down a child.

The television news talked about the biggest bankruptcy in the history of the U.S. now occurring. There was much of the world she needed to catch up on. She was ready.

Then she buzzed for Dr. Olden. As she awaited his arrival, she looked at her arms and ankles which still bore the scars from the badly padded manacles that had locked her to a corner of her floral wallpapered dark make-shift prison room.

"How could they have been so cruel to me?" she asked Dr. Olden, for the hundredth time.

She sat on the blue denim upholstered couch, he sat across the room from her on the matching easy chair wearing gray slacks, white shirt, a blue and gray thin striped tie and a white doctor's jacket, unbuttoned. His mostly white and gray hair still had some black strands, and his face still had the wrinkleless pink cheeks of a much younger man. He had hoped that she would burst through the dark cloud. Every patient is on their own time schedule for recovery. Some never do.

"It is usual that a person who inflicts torture finds respectability for doing it from the other members of their group. They rely on that. And in this case, they were trying to get specific information from you, so they had what they considered a purpose for the torture, to coerce you to give them the information that they wanted."

"But they didn't just torture me and hit me. They did unspeakable things to me. And they enjoyed it," she said as tears slid down her face.

"Unfortunately for you, it is true that they found a way to give themselves pleasure taking advantage of your being at their mercy. You have lived through every woman's worst nightmares. I know you will never really know how many times you were raped. That you survived as well as you did attests to the remarkable strength you had attained for yourself before all of this started. Because of that, you are luckier than most."

"I feel like I haven't had a good night's sleep in years," Amy told Dr. Olden, "with awful nightmares, and sweating and anger and fear all the time. I've even been afraid to listen to you. But I feel good right now. I feel like I am peaking from behind a dark curtain and there is the light."

Dr. Olden wanted to hug his patient but he knew that he had to keep his communication only verbal.

"I used the telephone today. I called Cortland. The call did not connect to him. I left a message with a machine."

"I'm glad that you wanted to speak with Cortland, Amy. He has been here almost every day. He cares for you so much."

"And he feels guilty, I'm sure. He knows that who he is, and what he does, is why I was kidnapped."

"That has not been easy for him to live with."

"Sometimes I think this whole experience must be an article I wrote, that all of this could not possibly have really happened to me. But then I look down and see the scars. And then the memories come back. My whole being cringes and everything becomes unbearable, it's hard to breathe." Then she was crying hysterically, her shoulders jerking up and down, her chest heaving. When she was able to catch her breath and wipe her nose, she said, "I thought I was cured. I didn't think I would cry like that again."

Amy took a few more deep breaths. When she was ready, she continued, "Am I going to be all right now, Dr. Olden?" She needed to know that he had an answer that she could hold onto.

"You've been devastated but you are pulling yourself together again. You will have flashbacks, regressions, post-traumatic stress. I know that you understand these concept emotionally and intellectually."

"I felt so strong just a few minutes ago. I can't believe I was so easily brought to tears," she said.

"Their torture was physical, but their goals were psychological. They wanted to break your will, to terrorize you, so that you would tell them what they wanted to know, and in your case you were also their hostage," he said. "Studies show that the fundamental neuro-chemical balance in the brain is actually altered by traumatic events. Now you're reconditioning your reactions back to normal will reconfigure the chemical balance in the brain. You have more control over your body and your mind than you think you do." Then he added, "you'll see. I promise you that you are going to be fine."

He paused to give her time to digest what was happening, and for him to decide if this was the time for him to tell her even more.

In the middle of that sentence there was a knock on the door, and before either Dr. Olden or Amy could say anything, Cortland was standing in the doorway.

CELL PHONE

She was walking down the street, on the sidewalk, of course, talking on her cell phone. So she wasn't paying enough attention to where she was walking and probably didn't realize that she was veering to the left, and then to the right, kinda gliding down the sidewalk talking attentively into her phone. I was walking behind her, it was such a pain it was as if I was walking behind a row of four people. Every time I tried to pass her she'd swerve my way, even though she didn't even know I was behind her.

I was all dressed up in my black outfit and pony tail with a new hair band that was a leopard print. Well, I'm always fashionable, I read Vogue, I watch Elsa Clench and I walk through Bloomingdales and Barney's and CVS so I know what's going on. I lied for a change and said I was going to meet Emma at the movies. I changed in the storage house where I always change.

But a girl? I had never done it to a girl, this could lead to chaos and anyway that's just not me. But I was mesmerized by her total lack of focused awareness to her surroundings. I imagined that she must be really in love with whoever she was talking to. So I decided that since I couldn't pass her, I could at least catch up to her and walk in tandem with her and maybe listen in to a little of the conversation, maybe pick up a few pointers.

I felt like the daughter of Secretariat at Cheshire Downs. The crowds were cheering, my sinuous muscles were kneading my bones as I slowly inched up to her strut and there we were, neck in neck just ambling down the sidewalk and much to my surprise I'll never really get over what I saw. She had no chest, that is it was flat, and there were lots of hairs peeking out of the vee neck shirt. And there was a little bulge in the pants where there wouldn't be if she was a girl. Holy mackerel Mercury wasn't in retrograde for me yet, now was it.

I am the luckiest person I've ever known. I knew I wanted to get to know this person but it just wasn't right but now it's perfect.

So I bumped right smack into him. Bham. He was startled from his telephone daze and so I said, "Woops, excuse me. Oh, I'm so sorry." Of course I said that in the most sincere apologetic girlish voice I could muster. And but *"mais oui"* he fell for it right away, *"tout suite ah monsieur c'est demage. Vous avez les beaux yeaux bleu, mon roi, mon dieu, mon ami vien ici."* Yeah I had practiced that a few times but tonight it came out better and with more feeling.

Startled him again with my *francais* so now he thought maybe I was this adorable sexy French girl and how could he resist that no matter who he was talking so hungrily to on the phone. Whoever it was might have made him really receptive to a gal like me right about now. Let's see what happens.

"Oh, okay, well I gotta go now. I'm glad we finally talked this out. Oh gee my battery is about to die." Then he paused to listen and cut in quickly, "Yeah, that battery light is blinking like crazy. I'll speak to you tomorrow." Pause again. "Yeah, baby, me too."

Then he looked at me and smiled. "You from France?"

"If you want me to be, *mon cher*," I said. Then I started to laugh, cutely of course. I wanted him to still have a crush no matter where I was from.

He's thinking about what to do or say, what moves to make with me. And I'm thinking about me. I'm really always just thinking about me, that's why I guess I put myself first and only hear the needs of my newest friends when I've brought them to total tears. See, that was about me again, when I bring them to tears, it's not really about them. I've read a few books, and especially stories in the newspapers so I know that with some killers, after they do it for the first time, they want to do it again. And again. Like me.

I saw a big fish on the Discovery Channel. This tall gorgeous black and white was swimming and gliding through the deep water surrounded by sub aqua greenery with dozens of varieties of remarkable looking marine animals shimmying by. This big one had his mouth wide open, while his eyes were pretending nothing special was happening. But all the while other fish were swimming in to this mouth, surmising, in their fishy way, that they were swimming through just another waterway. Then oops crunch.

Oops crunch. I didn't really mean to do it that way, but that's how it happened. They just come to me, like a bee swarms to the hive, like a river flows upstream.

"Do you want to know the truth or a lie," I asked, knowing all the while that he didn't care what he heard as long as he could take me home with him tonight.

CORTLAND COMING IN

Cortland abruptly left Stamford after first visiting Amy in the hospital the next morning, after being told by Dr. Olden yet again to expect Amy's recovery to be very slow, and after telling Amy that he would come to see her again in a few days. As he drove onto I95 at Exit 8, past the new weary looking over head train station, he knew where he had to go, where he had to be.

As he steered in and out of traffic in the GRETA issue 1999 bulletproof ordinary looking Dodge, he said, into the air, "call Brenner." He could hear the rings, then a voice that said, "repeat your request." Cortland said, "call Brenner." He was inundated with the mellow screeching sounds of cyber space plucking the cosmos. He knew that each beep and yelp was checking his vocal signature, otherwise the call would simply abort.

"Yo Cortland, what's up?"

"I'm coming in, Brenner. I need to. I need the rest, and I need the protection. Can you arrange it. I'm on my way to LaGuardia now. I'll be there in just over thirty minutes. I'll leave the car where the road turns into the terminal drive, have someone pick it up."

"Call you right back. What happened?"

"There has been movement on all fronts. Amy is struggling. Heywood's tormentor is about to corner himself. We still haven't figured out how all of those carved bodies are connected but we know that they are. It's still convoluted but you can see the logic beginning to take hold at the horizon. I think. I hope." He paused. That was all he was going to say right now, even on this secured line. "I look forward to your call."

Cortland tuned in to 1010 WINS, the all news all the time radio station to hear if any one had picked up any of the scents they had purposely left out there. They had intended to leave an unsparing trail, and they did. There were rumors spread in select white collar and government mole prisons, to the right street criminals, in the right corrupt organizations, leaks to the press, and in certain other circles. Within twenty-four hours the individual or group behind the threat to off the most important person behind the military and intelligence of our country would certainly hear the message. Somehow they were going to provoke them out in to the open.

THE MAN ON THE BUS

       I met you on the crosstown bus. I liked you because you remind me of my cousin George. He was also tall with such long legs he looked like a spider no matter what he did. You got all nervous when I wanted to sit next to you, I tried to calm you down by telling you I was looking for a seat not a relationship. Now you're lying there with your legs and arms flailing around you look more like a cockroach who's been kicked onto his back. If you were a bug I could just step on you but you're a long person and I just want to know how did I get so insane. They say admitting your problem is the first step towards recovery. I'm insane I'm insane. There. I admit it.

RITA CAFFEINE

If I drink any more caffeine, oh how I love my caffeine, just imagining myself on the other side of the park will get me there. What a time of year. The daffodils are in bloom, the crocuses are croaking, you can walk down the street eating an ice cream.

Yeah baby. Spring is in the air in the Northeast. Makes it easier to get around. Makes it seem more okay to be out and about. I would like to spend more of my free time out and about, and this way it will not be as notable as why do you want to spend so much time out when it's snowing or it's cold. Well of course I don't, but when I need my fix of fun, I do so I do.

I can't get sloppy here, I just can't. There is much too much at stake here. I like to be able to live the way that I live. Oh god I don't want to put any of it in jeopardy. I'm careful, I always am. I never ever leave anything anywhere that anyone could possibly look at askew.

I take the morning train into Penn Station it's never too crowded after rush hour. A little train ride, it's more anonymous than a car. What a day, it's a whole entire day outing, a day trip, I'm day-tripping. What, under an hour to the city. Dressed a little lady like today so I look like a commuter. What else I did not leave one thing out not one fucking thing.

Now going to Grand Central Station Metro North to Connecticut, Stamford, here I come. Just visiting, just need to go someplace different for a change. Just paying my respects to an old neighborhood. A really nice place. Yeah baby.

By the time I got to the station, I was sure I was going to miss the train. I'm never on time, especially if I have to be somewhere at like eleven oh five. They shouldn't be letting her out on her walks so soon, now should they.

So I ran and ran until I saw the round information booth in the middle of the enormous grand room of Grand Central Station, but there was a line so I looked up to the numbers that flip on the giant board on the wall and it said the Stamford train will leave from Track 23. I stopped at a kiosk and got a giant chocolate chip cookie, a bagel and cream cheese for the ride. I need nourishment and an activity I don't have the patience to just sit there. I brought a map of the town to study.

I have to figure out exactly what I'm going to pretend while I'm wearing my semi suburban gear of khaki pants, white tee shirt, navy blazer and penny loafers. Yes, I really look normal. Also a gold watch, navy and beige socks and a brown leather pocketbook.

I'd like a drink right now, that's what I would really like. Ahhh this is too much pressure. I should have done just my normal day trolloping and free associating until I did what I do best. We should all aspire to do what we do best, don't you think.

"Tickets please," said the train man working his way through the car with his paper punch with the cut-outs shaped like tiny little crooked stars, and the blue tickets.

"Where are you going, ma'am?"

"Stamford, sir."

He looked at his list and said, "That's fourteen dollars round trip off peak, seven fifty one way off peak. Will you be returning off peak, ma'am?"

Those were just too many questions all at

once. I didn't want to plan too far ahead so I said, "Uh just one way, please, sir." I'll get the other one when I travel back. That way I don't have to decide anything now.

And his response was punch punch, with little blue crooked stars falling to the floor.

I just want to sniff around town this trip, she thought, get an idea of where she is, so if need to really be here, I'll know exactly where to go.

AMY IN THE PARK

This time they let her leave the hospital alone. Well not really, she didn't know that she was being watched and protected at all times. She felt like a specimen so much of her life, growing up to be so beautiful, being kidnapped, having men play with her body and her soul until she wasn't sure if she was still there, brought back to civilization by doctors and nurses. They thought they knew her. They didn't.

She kept remembering what Dr. Olden said, 'you have to recondition yourself.'

The aide had left her alone for awhile, and so she walked down the street, away from the hospital towards her little house, a halfway move back to life. Cortland told her that her beach house was too dangerous to go back to, so it was locked and secured.

You can be alive and feel dead. She had been living in the scream.

The doctors and nurses had been wonderful, committed, professional, experienced, so sure that their courses of treatment were the right ones it usually felt safe but it was a different kind of captivity.

But Cortland. They had been in love. After months of treatment her memories started to return, from the horrible ones to the exquisite. How could it be that once she loved him, oh yes, he was her shining star. But the years went by, they're just a memory, and seems like memories travel far.

He is smart in the world he is in, she thought, but he is not smart in the world. He tried hard to keep it alive, visiting her often, meeting with doctors, expecting that they would be together again.

She started to feel dizzy and walked into the park that was on her right. It was a four block by four block field in the middle of town. It had lawns, a snack shop, a large man made pond. She decided to sit before the dizziness became a faint.

She sat on the green wood slatted painted bench with its brass fittings, and quickly put her head down between her knees. She wept quietly. Everything was overwhelming. Maybe she left the hospital too soon.

Slowly she raised her head and looked around. The lawn was so beautiful she decided to sit on it, even though she was wearing light khaki pants. There were teardrops also on the blades of grass. She put her head down and cried some more. A black butterfly with blue dots landed on her hand.

On the hilly lawn people were perched like birds. A glorious day, temperature in the 70's, the sky a perfect baby blue, no clouds.

She knew that her experiences were far out of the range of most mortals. She looked around some more. Forget the purple majesty, let's talk about the green majesty with that baby blue topping. It was more than enough to bring more tears to her eyes. Finally, the beginning of another time.

NEXT TRAIN

This morning I decided to take the 9:06 express into Manhattan. I had stayed in Stamford the night before. It was rush hour, so of course the train station in Stamford was crowded with Tuesday morning commuters. What an ugly station on a sunny day it looks like a cement slab that never dries. There used to be a colonial looking station on the same spot, it was green with white shutters. Sure the population exploded, but whose idea was it to go from lovely to slab.

I was lucky my favorite seat was available, on the end of the car, where two sets of seats face each other, like a little nesting. I hated sitting in the long row, everybody facing the same way, looking only at the backs of somebody's head. This way I had some air and space in front of my face, I could see down the whole car. And this way, I could meet up to three people and chat about the day's crossword puzzle, a commuter's amusement.

Usually sitting across from me was someone I was not too interested in talking to, but this time I was mesmerized by this man with a design of freckles on his hand that undulated with the movement of his fingers as they penned the answers to the puzzle. Just caught my eye. I thought I am more artistic than that,

114

I should show him, he'd appreciate it, so I started a conversation with him.

WALLPAPER

This was Amy's second time in the little house, the first was with an aide from the hospital who Dr. Olden wanted to accompany her for the first visit. Even though it was always obvious to a woman where the dishes and silverware were kept, it was nice not to have been alone the first time here.

My little house, my halfway house, my tip-toe peek-a-boo back to the world, was sweet. All I will ever want again is a place in the middle of the country where there is no ocean. But she loved the ocean.

Whoever picked it out knew that serenity was what I needed. I sat at the kitchen table and looked out the window and there, I couldn't believe it, was a large pond which I think they ordered from a Norman Rockwell painting because five ducks were swimming together and the green reeds along the edges were swaying so calmly I thought they would hypnotize me. It was early enough in the day that the morning glories were still open in their purple blue regalia.

The tiny bedroom had enough room for a single bed and a small dresser, but the pink blanket cover matched the pink carpet so I'm sure only girls ever lived here as they matched also the pink towels in the bathroom. Or did they do that just for me because things have been so rough, so harsh, so dark, so colorless. And look, even the couch has pink flowers on it, just like the wall paper in my cell, oh is someone playing a cruel joke on me I have to get out of here.

Amy ran back to the hospital, thankfully just a few blocks away, practically breaking the glass revolving door that wasn't moving fast enough and then racing down the hall to Dr. Olden's office oh my god please let him be here.

Dr. Olden was standing there with his white hospital coat on, holding a clipboard of another patient's particulars which he dropped when he saw Amy running towards him.

He grabbed her around her body as she crashed into him and cried, "what are they trying to do to me, what are they trying to do to me?"

"What's the matter Amy, what happened?" he asked as he quickly moved her to the cushioned chair in his office. Whatever happened, at least she had the where-with-all to come here, he thought.

STRAWBERRY FLOAT

I think I finally figured it out. Why I am the way I am, that is. It's raining out, but it's muggy. The windows are closed so I can't hear much outside noise. The air conditioning is on cause it's July and even though the utility company just raised their rates, this place is like an ice box so fuck them I don't pay the bills around here anyway. So what can I do. I can't run around in the rain so I'm here watching television and this really strange feeling just came over me about fifteen minutes ago. I thought what the hell is this feeling it's so unrecognizable as something I should readily recognize. So I thought I'd analyze it, cause I'm intelligent and I like to think things through especially because if anybody thinks I'm stupid that is cause for me to have an arts and crafts fit with my cute little carvers.

Okay, I need a drum roll here. What it is is...ta ta dum...dum dum dum... I'm relaxed. Yes, I'm fuckin relaxed. It's such a strange feeling cause this is the first time I'm relaxed in about ten years. Or fifteen years. Long enough ago that it is noticeable. I'm thinking too much lately. Now I'm worried.

Was there any evidence? Did I leave anything behind? I don't think so. I think that I am so thorough that only I know where I went and where

I'm going now.

I left them in their own homes. With the detritus of their own ridiculous lives. I could see right away, with each and every one of them that they were simply extras here, not necessary at all on this planet, and had not experienced anything really important and ultimate. Which of course I could give them better than anyone. I could see the adoration and thanks in their eyes, even though such gratefulness isn't always easy to put into words. Sometimes merely a look can say it all.

Okay another one down the drain, maybe a pun intended, sure I'm so clever. He was resting so peacefully in the tub, surrounded by a strawberry float of these really gorgeous pink bubbles pouring out of my carving drippings, so many that there must have been at least a million trillion of them. Looked good enough to drink.

Time to go home. It's just that I'm tired tonight and I don't want to forget anything. My hair band is on firmly, my black long sleeve tee shirt was only off for a few minutes when he was sucking on me but I put it back on as soon as I had disabled his tongue. Oh, I wrote 'My Name Is Rita' with a red pentel pen on the cover of his new issue of Vanity Fair magazine. I chose that because on that particular cover was a picture of the year's best actors, I wish I could meet every one of them, and so, okay, I put my signature there.

But I'm just so tired. Maybe it was because I did so much at the house. I don't usually do that much. But I got energetic. I just couldn't stop. Spring fever, I guess. I changed closets. Put the summer clothes downstairs, and brought the winter clothes to the upstairs closets. The house is so god damn big what a pain. But it was very therapeutic. I realize so much when I am doing physical labor. You know, little epiphanies here and there, and some really big light bulbs exploding in your head. It is so important to realize what it's all about.

Then it was time to go out, how much can you stay in and do when it is so beautiful outside and there are so many interesting people to meet. It's important to have an interesting life, you only live once.

Okay, I look good, ponytail in place, soft-soled sneakers on, a little lipstick, rouge and off I go.

CARA AND CERISE SHOP

I better hurry because she'll be here soon. I showered, put on my make-up, slipped into my silk underpants, chocolate brown pants outfit and my brown suede loafers with the pretty thick gold chain on the rim. I really like cotton underpants but you can't wear them when you're going shopping to try on dresses and pants. You just can't. I look so scrubbed and fresh. Cerise would never guess what I've already done today. She just would never. Who would, let's face it, I'm a genius.

Belinda, where are you. You didn't iron my blouse enough. You didn't organize my dressing table. Where is that blush-on.

Honk honk, there she is pulling up the driveway to my mansion. Crunch crunch goes the gravel, bark bark go the dogs. I better look in the mirror and check everything one more time. When we have it, we spend it. Love to shop, love my number one and only husband to see the results of my having fun shopping. It's his payoff to me, it's my pleasure to get paid back for the shame I'm supposed to feel for all of his cheating on me. He feels so guilty, I know he suffers from his guilt. It takes up so much of his time thinking about me that he has no idea what I do. No idea ever. He thinks I'm the same girl he married. He's right, I am. But he didn't know me then, and he doesn't know me now. Where is my Oscar, my Tony, my Emmy. I want one, I do. But my husband and I, we are both so busy fooling the other that neither one of us has any idea what's really going on here. We're the perfect match. Which is fine with me. I have to be myself.

I know that I just get into these crazy wacky moods sometimes, can't be the same monotone self all the time.

Honk honk, okay okay here I come. For such a classy lady, she is sure an impatient honker. Who knew. Her husband is more the kind I should have married, a man of blue blood and position. But she likes me anyway, she always has since the first time we met at a cocktail party. Maybe I'll run into her husband one day and see what it's like being with a man like that, I mean really being with a man like that. Hold nothing back, really take him to the max. To the sax, to the bax, the fax, lax, rax, tax, wax, the hax, ha ha, no pun intended. But then she might move and I won't have my best shopping friend any more. Can't risk that. Too much of a loss.

I flew out the door with my three-quarter length mink. My hair was loose, newly colored but not styled, just straight and wildly perfect. She was just about to say, "Cara, you look so great." But I told her to shut up, under my breath of course, for what she surely was thinking.

By now I was outclassing her with my every outfit, my every witty word. The next stop was her man, I know it, she knows it now. It was the scent on me, the scent of me. I was a satisfied woman, and I smelled like one.

"Cara, my dahling," Cerise said. "You do look wonderful today. There's something different, you really put it together today." She watched my face, waiting for me to break the spell and act like my normal self again but I wouldn't break character. I could sense she was getting more and more frustrated and wanted to have the chance to take another shot at me. I knew the light bulb went off for her when she realized how she could get more in my face time before we lost each other trying on clothes.

Cerise turned to me, her blonde hair shining so straight and perfectly cut a few inches past her chin, the bangs just rolling over her eyes. "Have you had lunch yet, Cara? I'm famished, sorry. Meant to grab something before I left the house but I simply couldn't. The phone. The phone just kept ringing and I kept getting side tracked." She looked to see my reaction. "You are hungry too, aren't you?"

"Oh, I am. I'm always hungry." Before she could wonder what I really meant by that I added, "Let's eat at the restaurant upstairs in Neiman Marcus at the mall."

Cerise agreed. She always agrees with me. She loves my small talk probably because she doesn't have any. "Belinda is driving me crazy," I started. "Lately she hasn't been putting my things where they're supposed to be, I can never find anything when I need them, including her. I don't know where she is half the time. But I can't fire her. She's mostly good, and I feel like she knows my family too personally by now. Do you know what I mean?"

"Of course I do," Cerise answered. "Until a few years ago I could never keep help for more than a year, for the house, for me, there was always something. Until the last one, she completed the picture for me, you know, kept the house perfectly clean, kept my things, the wash and dry cleaning in order. She is good and honest and thorough and she helps me watch over the house. I really can't complain."

"Well, Belinda is good most of the time. Except sometimes she seems to just disappear. I know I give her a lot of errands to do. But I was looking for my ironed blouse, I'm looking for my blush-on and a few lipsticks on my dressing table. Some things just seem to vanish for awhile. And all of a sudden there she is with everything done perfectly. Perfectly. So what am I supposed to do, I don't want to complain about little things. And I don't have the patience to look for someone new."

THE THIRD FLOOR

The rays of sunshine burst out of the sky like the way the sunshine surrounds Moses in every picture of him carrying the Ten Commandments. In this case it was the prismed sparkles of lights created by my squinting eyes as I tried so desperately to conjure the future. I want it to be a bright future, and if this were any prelude, all I had to do was squint and a light and lovely world was there.

But if I didn't squint, if I just looked at the world the way it was, not so bright and cheerful.

I refluffed the red velvet pillow behind my head as I sat in the window seat on the third floor of the house. It was so quiet up here, most of the time most don't remember it's even there. I could 'disappear' by being up here for days before anyone might think of it. I had a stash of canned food, manual can openers, plastic plates and cups. The only problem with hiding for any length of time was if I had to flush the toilet. Would need to be creative there.

Why was I even thinking about this. Why would I need to spend so much time there. My schedule was too busy to have so much relaxing time away from the world. Although something about the thought was inviting. Maybe the voices would stop, with their awful demands on me. Not voices like you hear nuts have. My voices were different. They were sweet, whispering catnip I couldn't resist.

It had just a square little window facing the back of the house.

LITTLE SUGAR BOMBS

"Gimme some of those little sugar bombs, please," I asked in my sweetest voice. As I hoped, he thought that was adorable, my referring to those cute jelly beans that way. I thought it was pretty clever myself. If he thinks that's cute, wait till he finds out how really precious I can be.

I am sometimes so ashamed and embarrassed to be me, I can't take me anywhere. I have done so many stupid things, made so many mistakes, acted hastily when I should have taken more time, I have taken more time when I should have acted hastily.

Wasn't it yesterday, I thought, that life seemed so simple. Sometimes it's all in black and white, and sometimes it's in Technicolor. Sometimes you're watching it, and sometimes you're in it. I am always all of the above at the same time. That's just me, nothing special.

"Hey, my lady," said Ray. "Would you like to have a drink while you're eating your little candies?"

I watched him walk towards the bar that he had custom made for his living room. He had everything: wine, liquor, liqueurs, and a little hidden refrigerator with sodas and juices that had a little machine that made tiny spherical ice cubes. Ray was tall, about 6 feet, the kind of good looking that probably was once gorgeous, but now he's older and a little paunchy. His hair is thinning, with a little gray striped through it. That part was sophisticated; the part that aged him was the beginning of an extra jowl on his face. But still there was that something about him. He had authority, he was expensive.

"Sure, I'd love a vodka with cranberry juice, hold the vodka, no lemon, no lime," I said. He looked at me puzzled.

"It took us such a long time to get here," he said, trying to convince me to have a drink with liquor in it. If that was the best he could come up with, where were we going to go from here.

He was wearing a red shirt. That was no good. I had to make him change so I devised a plan.

"Ray, listen." I waited until I had his complete attention. I've been holding this in too long. There was something about his eyes. The way they looked at me. The way I felt when his hand held mine for just that minute when he had first walked me into this living room. I have never felt so safe. I have never felt so understood. I have to tell him. Maybe I'll even tell him everything, then I'll be okay, and then, and then I can let him be okay. Maybe. No Happy Valentine's Day Baby Bye Bye for him. Maybe. Am I just imagining all this because things have been a little boring lately? Or is he really that special.

Is that why I get dizzy when I try to go down a down escalator, especially if it is a long escalator, on a certain angle, especially if I'm wearing heels but sometimes even with sneakers. That, I think, is when all of my neurosis totally come to the surface, when I am approaching a down escalator. That's my only fault, really. Otherwise I am a perfectly normal and healthy human being.

It's true, I am, cause I have a great attitude, and attitude is everything. Although they also say that looking good is the best revenge. Okay I have both of those.

I babble sometimes, because I have an extremely active imagination. It just doesn't stop, these stories in my head. I asked a shrink once if I was schizophrenic. I told him that I was living on so many different planes at the same time, an outer world and an inner world, and sometimes they melded, but sometimes they didn't. But he said no. Maybe if that one had realized what the real story was, everything would have been different. I think. I don't know, those little balsa wood carving knives sure inspire me. I can't imagine living without that creativity.

I watched his face to see if he was really listening. I could tell that he was, especially when he said, "What, baby. What do you want me to listen to." What more did I need than that?

"Ray, there's something I need to tell you. Because I already feel so close to you. Well actually, there are a few things I have to tell you."

"I'm listening, baby. I'm listening. I could watch your beautiful face talk to me forever. Tell me what's on your mind."

Oh oh. I had to be sure. If he got scared, he could do something to hurt me. My life is confusing enough. What was I doing. Somebody could get very hurt here. Emotionally, physically. I don't know what I mean anymore. And if I tell him a few things, will he suggest taking me home or want to keep me here. What will happen to everything. If he just holds me for awhile, maybe everything will be alright.

COLTER AND GRANGE

The stories were terrifying everyone in the New York and the tri-state area. Mutilated bodies couldn't be kept secret for too long. The local precincts were stymied and the press, while crazed, was trying to do what was right by taming the roar. Colter and Grange didn't know why, but the investigations were being conducted by the Feds, so all they could do was gather whatever came their way and turn it over to them.

New York City Detective Colter phoned Detective Grange, his cohort in solving some of the city's more momentous crimes. They relished talking about all the smut going on, even if it wasn't their case.

"What do you think, Grange, why are they keeping this from us."

"I don't know for sure," responded Colter, 'But I want to talk about this more but not on the phone. Wanna meet me at the Varsity Grill in about an hour?" It was only 11:30 a.m., so that was perfect.

The Varsity Grill was on West 54th Street, right in the neighborhood where all of the music business offices used to be before they moved downtown. The Grill was where all the musicians and record executives used to go for lunch and dinner and at three in the morning when they left the recording studios. Now the patrons were the local cops, garmentos, writers, neighborhoodies and only the occasional music and theater type.

"If you see two of these, three of these, you know it's a serial sicko and if we just keep on the trail they'll mess up and we'll get them," Colter said with his usual logic as he started on his first cup of coffee while they were waiting for the best, tallest, meatiest, meanest pastrami sandwich in Manhattan. Colter's sandy hair was swinging by his eyes as he focused on Grange sitting across from him.

"But why the Feds, why? Local people doing local things, sure this is creepier than most but where's the national concern?" Grange wondered out loud.

"The most I've heard so far is this. They think that maybe ya' know, maybe someone was seeing someone in a way they shouldn't have. I mean an affair. An affair gone bad – really really bad. And someone flipped out and some crazy people are involved," Colter tried to explain.

"I know it sounds convoluted," he continued, "but that's the most I can make sense of the rumors I've been hearing."

"But usually, even in a case like this, they want to involve us at least on the street level cause these are our streets and no one knows them better than us," stated Grange.

"Well we'll just have to keep listening so that we'll know what to do when they call us, which I have a feeling is going to happen."

TWO BOYS IN QUEENS

They were eight years old and lived down the block from each other in Flushing, Queens, NY in a row of attached post World War II low-cost three story houses that in Manhattan were called townhouses that were later worth millions.

They started talking one day on the playground after Heywood took a fall, sports weren't one of his talents, and Tony had pulled him up fast just as the other kids started to tease him for his clumsiness. After that, they usually walked to school together and had fun questioning everything they could think of, but it was clear that Douglas Heywood had the brains and Tony Camera had the nerve so they complimented each other in a divisive way. That's how it started, that's what lead Heywood to invite him home for cookies after school one day.

After a few months he let Tony take a peek into the little playroom that his father had fabricated for him on the side of the basement, using the two support polls as guides for the plywood walls, with the closeable opening that Heywood had asked for. He had projects, but he wanted to do them in a secluded way so that he could concentrate, he already had so much on his mind. Some days he hinted to Tony about his projects, his inventions, but he never told him too much, he was very secretive. Tony asked about them, he wanted Heywood to think he was smart like him. Even at those young ages, Heywood only shared what he felt was innocuous, he was protective and guarded, he always thought he was onto concepts that could change the way things worked in the world.

After several years of walking together, and becoming dependent on each other for so many things that seemed so critical at the time, one day Tony wasn't on his stoop where he usually waited for Douglas to start their walk to school. The next day he wasn't there either. Douglas soon heard that Tony's parents had been killed in a car accident and Tony had no choice but to move away to live with his aunt and uncle.

LOSING PATIENCE

"I'm losing patience. The most intriguing cases I ever hear about, in my thirty years of doing this, come from the New York City area. Never fails," chuckled Grange as he picked up his off-white thick coffee cup handle and sipped his fourth cup of black wake up juice since breakfast and it was only one in the afternoon.

"Look," responded Colter. "I know it seems that way, especially in times like this." Grange looked up from his paper messy desk, across the room to where Grange's desk was facing his own. "How can we help, we are looking at probably the hardest case we've ever had to face."

Colter stopped talking, not really meaning to, but his own response was cause for pause. He rarely worried because there would always be a crack in the siding and he would start seeing what's inside. But not with this one. Whoever was perpetrating this string of maniacal killings was not only out of his mind but intent on being his version of artistic. Very strange. And time after time he left no clues. Nobody leaves no clues.

Colter slid his legs up towards the desk top, crossed them at the ankle and rested the heels of his feet right on the wooden covered metal desk, and then continued.

"Well, we've got forensics on every case, every print, every piece of DNA, every hair, every particle, but so far nothing." He looked up and shook his head from side to side, not being able to hide the disbelief he was feeling.

"We've been tracing all their contact lists and address books, relatives, business associates, their friends, schools, travels. Nothing. How can it be nothing. This has been going on for too long."

Grange picked at the pencil eraser falling off the desk and listened as Colter kept talking.

"How can there be no footprints, nothing on a glass, nothing in a bathroom, nothing on the floor, no prints from the blood, no hair, no fibers. This person is stealth. No person is stealth, this is impossible."

"We've had people we couldn't find for years. But we had something to go on," added Grange.

"Let's hit harder at international," Colter said as he sprung to his feet. "I know we've had the dispatch out there for years, but we need to come up with a new strategy, this can't sit still any longer."

"You're right. We've never had a situation like this. What is it about the person doing this that they can elude us, we're the best, we're New York. It doesn't make sense." He thought a bit and then added, "Maybe they're purposely not sharing information with us. Let's call MI-6 and Interpol — let's see if we can get even a crumb."

COLTER AND INTERPOL

I'm not about to go to France, Colter thought, and I don't need to. We're New York, we have people all over Europe all of the time. We would know.

That's when the call came in.

"It's Interpol U.S. Services," Colter's assistant Evan relayed, after he answered the ringing phone on his desk just outside Colter's door and beeped Colter's secure phone three beeps indicating an urgent call.

"Thank you, I'll take that call right now," Colter said as he readied himself for anything he might hear.

"We had a murder reported just up the hills from Nice," the Captain from Interpol U.S. Services told Colter. "Unusual for this part of the world," he continued. After a brief pause he added, "One of our men just returned from New York and has a friend in your precinct who told him about a few of the cases he was working on. Our man said it had similarities to a case you had that was on the cold side."

"Yes," Colter agreed, "unfortunately we do have cases like that. And if you're referring to the one I think you might be, that has been particularly bothersome because it is not at all the type of case that we wouldn't normally solve within days. But we don't have commanding jurisdiction on this one."

Colter shook his head. This has been one of the most depressing cases of his thirty year career, and wouldn't it be so unexpected to be solved like this.

He had to know. "What's the M.O.," he asked his international colleague.

"It were the carvings on the lad's abdomen that caught the attention of our investigators, sir."

"What kind of carvings? Orbs? Musical notes?"

"No, it was flowers."

"Did you get in touch with our Feds," Colter asked.

"Yes of course, I wasn't to contact you until that was done. They said you'd understand."

DANCING WITH AMY

I couldn't imagine dancing any closer, Colter thought. Any closer and we would be walking through each other. What a moment to remember at a time like this.

Just three years ago Amy and I had gotten all dressed up for our anniversary. I was wearing my new tuxedo with the shapely satin lapel crescenting two and a half inches wide to the single button. She was wearing a baby blue three layer chiffon skirt French length to her knees. Stunning. We were a stunning sight. I loved her so. Our second anniversary. I would give her a ring in a few months. That night we danced and fell even more in love. All that was good in life was for all eternity. Forever ended just a few weeks later.

Now she behaves the way you imagined a lot of people did after they had experienced Janov's therapy in the 70's, or was he still doing that, I wasn't sure. He brought his patients back to their birthing experience. Now Amy is new and vulnerable like that again, but she is also so abused. So afraid. So thick with scars that know no peace.

She looked so beautiful, even though her beauty now wasn't as disarmingly soft and warm and magnetic as it used to be because she was now armored in her own self protective shell. She seemed like a tired deer who had stood paralyzed staring into the headlights for a year too long. This was her first time truly going out for an entire evening since she had left the hospital, dressed up, in a car, in a restaurant with strangers and a menu and choices and music. I took her in my arms as the maitre'de scanned the room for our table and the captain.

She looked so scared and stoic. She looked so sad and tentative. I had dreamed so many days and nights that we would find Amy and she and I would have a night out. Like this. I was a man who could cry. I cried, after pretending I was so strong and regimented. Brenner was right. He knew my weakness. He knew that my emotionalism would have encumbered finding Amy. It was there in my brain waves, it was in my eyes, and in the subtle drop in the pitch of my voice. It was there.

"Amy."

She melted into my arms. Maybe she will be okay again.

TV SERIES

Look. I have to tell you this. I am not who you think I am. Almost, but not quite. Really, you have to listen to me or you won't see what's happening, like if you miss an episode of a television series – you just can't miss anything.

REGA AND CARA DINE

Where's Belinda. She always knows what to do. "Belinda, Belinda! Where are you?" Caranina pleaded to the air. She didn't know for sure what to wear. She wanted to dress just right. It had been too long since they'd gone out to dinner, out on a date, out as man and woman, away from his men and the house, acting like they were still an item. What should she wear.

Belinda appeared in the doorway just then looking haggard, like she just ran two miles and was sweaty with her eye make-up smudged from the dripping perspiration.

"Gees, where have you been Belinda. Sorry to say it, but you look like a dog who tried to run away."

"I'm sorry Miss Caranina, I'm sorry. I had a family emergency that I had to take care of. I should have left you a note. I'm sorry." She looked at my face for approval, then didn't wait for any and just continued. "What can I help you with?"

She never leaves a note, I thought to myself, why would this time be different.

"Mr. Rega and I are going out tonight. You of all people know how long it's been. I need to decide what to wear. I've been looking for my red dress with the single shoulder and I can't find it anywhere. Do you know where it is?"

"Yes, yes, I'll be right back." She left the room and ran down the stairs.

After about ten minutes she was back with the dress hanging in a dry cleaners' plastic bag. In the meantime I had found the matching red shoes and evening bag methodically arranged on a shelf in the back of my closet where I kept all of the matching accessories perfectly lined up so that I could easily see what exactly goes with what. No thinking, no fretting, there it all was matchy matchy. The reds, the blues, the golds, the plain, the sparkles, the day time things, the evening things, all laid out for my luxurious appreciation and ease of dressing.

I'm such a spoiled brat and I know it. But I'm a good kid, so it's ok. I'm loved, I'm appreciated. What if it's cold in the restaurant maybe I need a wrap, so I took one.

Wow, I thought to myself when I looked in the mirror. Wow. He's going to fall in love with me all over again. That's good, but really so what. So what. What would that change for more than a day it's happened before.

I could hear him coming up the stairs. "Hi honey, I'm here, I'm home, it's me. Are you ready?"

He walked into my room and just like I knew he would he said, "Wow. My Caran. Look at my girl, look at my baby. You make my heart pound so hard. Give me your hand." He was wearing his usual black: a black evening suit with a black silk shirt and black silk tie, black shoes and black socks. This is what he loved. It was always perfect with his black hair, what could be better.

He had made reservations at our favorite restaurant, New York Prime in Manhassat.

The driver let them off at the front entrance, and although she did not drink often, Caran agreed to have a Cabernet with him while he had his usual scotch on the rocks.

She looked gorgeous, she knew it, but she wasn't herself, and it was impossible for him to realize the extent of it. Does he realize something's askew?

Can he see it in her face, now that he is really looking at her for the first time in a long time.

And then came the big surprise. The huge unexpected. The big mayonnaise. "My precious, I think you and I should go away. We need a vacation. Together. Just you and me." He watched for her reaction and it finally came in the form of she practically spit the red wine out of her mouth and all she could think of was that it was a good thing that she was wearing a red dress.

But she said, "Rega, Rega, do you really mean it. We haven't gone away in too long. I think Acapulco, at Las Brisas, was our last vacation. Where would we go, what are you thinking?"

"I'm thinking of Florida, South Florida. We fly into West Palm and stay on the water at one of those pretty hotels. You can go to the spa and the beach. We can have dinner like this every night, maybe even go dancing a little." He watched her face for more reaction, a smile, but she looked at him as if she was waiting for him to tell her what, the truth? "What do you say?"

Something was going on was what she was thinking now. Things were just too weird at the house lately, something was in the air, something that he was micromanaging. To just go away all of a sudden. She wasn't totally sure what it was all about, but she knew that he was furious at someone or something and did this have something to do with that and the strange men in and out at the house lately. Oh, and this is why he asked her out tonight. Not because he was interested, not because he wanted to heat things up again, not because of something about the two of them. She knew it.

"When?" she asked.

"Tomorrow."

REGA AND CARA TRAVEL

Rega walked through the kitchen and down the long hall and outside, across a path which lead to a fancy barn that was his temple where he went to find peace. When he opened the door, there were his treasures. A 1965 Carroll Shelby Cobra, an original that was purchased for him by a proxy. It was deep gray, with a wide white stripe down the center, a single roll bar, no top, no air conditioning, no heat, no radio, the most beautiful carved metal gas and brake pedals, and it was as loud as ten motorcycles but it was a dream of a roadster. And he had a 1957 turquoise Thunderbird with hot fins and a grill that smiles at you. And his pride, a 1959 Jaguar 3.4 small sedan, with stately curved fenders, sky blue exterior with oxblood leather and wood interior.

They took the Delta Flight leaving from La Guardia at 1:35 in the afternoon, first class to Palm Beach which has the most civilized lovely airport, what other airport could you call lovely. They flew as Mr. and Mrs. Carl Shores and so did their credit cards.

Security checked their bags for deadly devices, but when they got on the plane they were given serrated knives to cut the food, wasn't that a weapon.

He spent half his time on the phone, listening

and ordering people around, for what she was never sure. Didn't feel like this trip was going to be much different. I was falling asleep, I was thinking thinking and then ba boom, I thought we just bumped into a cloud.

I like the window seat, I still love looking at the clouds and the little buildings and people.

When they arrived in sunny Florida the driver collected their bags. With not even a day's notice, she and Belinda had gone into manic mode getting everything ready. Belinda wanted to go on this trip, but Caran decided that this time she could stay home, take some time off, take care of her own life.

Cara never really knew how Rega earned his money, only that he always had a lot of it. He was fierce about bringing money in all the time, that's what mattered to him, he was always sure that someone owed him for something, he was so proud of living big and having a great black wardrobe. Except when he was in the tropics he surprised himself and everyone who knew him and sometimes wore dashing colors.

HOTEL WITH GOLDEN ORBS

Ok, Florida, here we come. Finally. Oh those palm trees. Oh that ocean. Oh those cute little lizards that run around all over the place all of the time. Oh the red snapper, and oh yum the stone crabs. Hope there is a nice veranda facing the ocean so that I can watch for shark fins.

When Rega and Caranina checked into The Grand, the gorgeous hotel and spa right on the ecru beach, they were taken to a two bedroom villa at the end of a long pathway. Most all of the furnishings were white. No spaghetti marinara in this room please.

They were both wearing white slacks and coincidentally orange blouses, orange like a salamander before it crawls under the moss. Colorful Florida. The bellman had taken the bags into the bedroom and then fussed around the living room doing what Cara didn't see. But with no fanfare suddenly there was a loud pop. Oh my god they found us she thought as she started to run out of the room.

"Cara. It's champagne. Champagne for my Cara," Rega said as he ran to grab her and hold her to him.

"We're in Florida. We're away. We're on vacation," he said as he let her go. "And look at us –

we look so Florida, so tropical. Wouldja look at us. We've waited too long to go away together again. I think we haven't done this for a few years. It's my fault, I know it. It's always my fault. I get so busy, ya know, I want to keep you in style, I want you to always have everything you want." He looked around and out the sliding doors. "Jees we've needed to be far away from all that shit, even if it's only for a few days, huh hon, don't you think so. Aren't you happier now."

"Yes Rega, this is making me very happy."

"Why don't I fix us a little welcome drink." He walked over to the bar and took the bottle out of the stainless steel ice bucket. "There's the cool bottle of champagne," he peacocked, "just waiting for us with chilled glasses. For me and my Cara."

"Let me unpack a few things, Rega. I'll be right back." Cara hung up a few of her outfits in her walk-in closet that could be someone's little office, and put her toiletries in what was her white marble bathroom. The right side of the tub was walled by glass bricks coming up to a window with an endless view of ocean and sky. Didn't I need this, sure I do, she thought to herself. I need this, I need diamonds, I need a lobster, I need to be alone.

Rega opened the sliding doors and chivalrously took two glasses of champagne outside where the humid air immediately made his armpits sweat but he didn't say anything he wanted to be romantic. He set them on the wrought iron glass topped low table, went inside to get the platter of cheese and crackers, caviar, lobster and shrimp for two and waited for Cara to join him.

She sashayed out in a tropical delight that you could only wear when you are on a holiday, a long flowing skirt with a tightly fitted top all of clear and silver threads, so clear that you could mostly see through it. Rega had just turned around to say something to her and then when he saw her he couldn't talk. Until he could, and then he said, "Oh jees, jees Cara. Look at you. Every time I think you're incredible, you're more incredible. How can you do this to me? I can't believe it."

"Champagne for my lovely. A toast to us," he said.

How could he say that so sincerely and then go fuck another women. But here we are, she thought. There must be a reason he took me away. There must be a reason we're here, in this place. There must be a reason why we are still together. Oh yes. I'm in such a bad mood, I wish I wasn't here, I actually have a headache from the car and the flight and the limo. First class is nice. This room is nice. I would rather be doing something else.

Florida. I used to visit friends here, Cara thought. There are interesting communities. I like the country club communities best, I have friends who live in them. When I would visit them I'd think that this is like visiting your friends in summer camp - with twenty-five tennis courts, two golf courses, five pools, three restaurants, shows, singing, dancing, swimming, everything but water skiing – but no woodsy camp cabins here these are really nice bunks.

"Cara. Cara. Where are you, I've been talking to you."

"Oh Rega, I've just been thinking about how wonderful you are to take us to such a fine place. I couldn't have asked for more." He hugged her, she hugged him and he put a glass of champagne in her hand.

So gallant he was, standing there looking victorious in front of her, the man who provides all of this for her, the man who keeps her in her castle, but he forgot to build a moat.

"Let's toast. Let's toast to that I have the most beautiful, the sweetest, the most loyal wife in the world." They clicked glasses and sat on the white silk cushioned rattan chairs. They drank their champagne. And then he poured a second glass for them both.

They partook of the sumptuous platter of hors d'oeuvres, and she dabbed her lips with the hotel's white and gold printed napkins. G, it had a gold letter G, for The Grand, of course. And then she saw it, her eyes riveted to a most exquisite design –

there was a golden orb circled with a gold and silver ring, on the upper right corner. When her gaze left the napkin, she noticed that the same design was on the champagne glasses, and on the Limoges cheese plate, on the silver, and on the corner of the seat cushions.

All was quiet. The ocean came in and out with a melodic rush of millions of years of dead fish bones and pulverized coral reefs.

TANGA TANGA

There was this small little known town called Tanga Tanga, at the very western patch of Florida that no one noticed unless you know it's there or you happen to fly over it which rarely happened and you would have no idea what you were seeing anyway. There were no roads that an untrained eye could see it was so covered with brush and pine and uninviting foliage. But if you got there what you saw was pretty shocking, unless nothing much surprised you.

There were structures that looked like old trees that had simply fallen on other trees that simply could no longer hold themselves up – a clever camouflage invented by someone but it was never clear who.

I was never allowed to specifically go there, and how I got there is another story. But for now, I walked into this mess of trees laying askew and ascutter on the ground. I sat on one of them for a minute or more, I just needed to look around so that I could really appreciate that I was finally there.

Terence was nearing his retirement. He had been the behind the scenes confidant of so many highly placed secret government operatives, but there was still so much he wanted to know. He wanted to make sure that he visited every secret site that he had heard about. He knew that the cave was near here somewhere, and this was as close as he was ever going to get. If anyone ever saw me dressed like this, he mused, they would never have believed it was me. Even though I was the nation's top courier, and knew far more than I was supposed to know, I wasn't supposed to know about this.

CARA AND REGA EAT OUT

I dressed up market, my Rega is only happy when he feels rich, looks rich, and is rich. He likes me glamorous, well so do I. I wear clothes really well, always have. Put on one of my outfits by Yves Saint Laurent, love everything of Yves.

We'll eat at La Flamingo, the Five Star restaurant on the ocean in Boca Raton, Florida. It is only a half hour drive from where we are staying and of course it is the best, and of course all Rega has to do is call and we get one of the best tables.

La Flamingo is magnificent, of course it is. And I look exquisite, while Rega looks marvelous in his New York black, this time black silk slacks with moderate pleats and a black silk long sleeve blouse with his chunky but tasteful gold necklace and black snake loafers with a very small solid gold chain before the tongue. We're in Florida, no socks.

My Yves was a tangerine orange that lit me up and made the air in the room dance. Matching shoes with gold threads, leather pocketbook with gold threads. Elegant and stunning.

Who was I kidding. This is a charade, as Audrey would put it.

I have to know what's going on. He's been his usual adorably cool loving self, but there's been another layer, you can tell by the way he looks away when he normally wouldn't.

He had the use of a 2017 C7 Corvette, dark gray with sparkles exterior, gray leather interior, and a really fun OnStar, phone and radio. I push the 60s button, I love the girl groups, oh weren't they the best, and I love Sinatra, Dean and Tony too.

Geeees, why am I thinking so much, I hate it when I think this much. You have to function from your gut, from your innards, they tell you what's really going on.

While I was thinking I had a thought, that what if what is going on is going to make us a lot of money. That's probably what it is. But there have been strange people hanging around.

TEA AT FOUR

He could always create a secure line wherever he was, it was part of what you knew how to do if you were GRETA

"Heywood, we're getting closer."

"Delighted to hear that, my friend."

But Cortland had been watching the news, and he was not pleased that Heywood's daughter Samantha had started to go out again with her society friends. She was smarter than that, Heywood and Lyla were smarter than that. Why was this happening.

"I know what you want to say to me. She was invited to art gallery openings and dinner parties. It is nearly impossible to say no to her all of the time, although to her credit she has been policing herself as much as we have. She is too old to just sit home with her parents, day in and out. I had to let her attend a few events so that she could feel like herself."

"Well, perhaps it is for the good, it looks to the outside like all are behaving without fear and with normalcy. But still..."

"The guards are always there with her."

"One more thing," Cortland insisted. He had to get to the main point of his call. "What was the name of your partner when you first started in the high tech world."

"I didn't have a partner then. I've never had a partner. I'm not sure what you are getting at Cortland."

"Can we have tea this afternoon at around four?"

"Of course my friend, of course. I look forward to seeing you then."

REGA DARLING

"Rega darling," I purred, as we were having such a romantic night. We were dancing, slow dancing, all alone in our villa with the curtains closed and the ceiling window showing us the night sky with a few stars and a bit of moon.

"Yes my Cara, I like to make you happy, you are happy now I feel it. I feel it in my heart and in all of me." He was just so perfect sometimes. No matter how bizarre our relationship most often was, there was something about him, and there was always something about me and him together, it was irresistible.

Added to that was I love being in Florida with him. The warmth, the beach, the ocean – it is all so sexy. And our own nice size villa with full hotel services and amazing restaurants right here on the property and many more just a short limousine ride away.

On this night my color is turquoise: a silky flowy pant with a silk sleeveless vee neck blouse, turquoise ring, bracelet and necklace. I was nice and tan, what a perfect canvas I was for this. And Rega loved it, he ate me up.

Which was good because we both seriously needed to be distracted from our real every day lives.

What he was caught up in I wasn't exactly sure – I knew that something was different, something was heavy, something was weighing on him. Some things he confided in me, some things he didn't. Well, duh, I was that way too with him.

By now, whether we were actually in love any more or not, after all these years we did know each other really well – I knew his walks, with a repertoire of rhythms depending on if he was working or socializing. I knew his moods. I fell for him, but luckily after he had already fallen for me.

But why are some of his boys down here, we were supposed to be on vacation, just the two of us and a bodyguard hidden where we could reach him if we wanted to and if it was urgent that he needed us.

MURDER WITH A SMILE

I don't know how many times I've walked around this circle but I've been walking around this circle for a while now.

We are all just babies – don't you get it yet. It's just that our bodies get bigger and grow older, but that does not mean that we do too. I know that I for one am still infantile in too many ways.

I was driving the car they gave me this morning and I swear it's like driving around in a big loaf of bread with that bar code on it going through the sensor – ka-ching – to let me in. I'm always more concerned about getting out.

I have done everything they have asked of me and more.

But now I am trying to walk down the street and be like everyone else, I don't want anyone to notice me, I want to blend in.

At first she looked so sophisticated and well manicured wearing all beige – slacks, knitted top, jacket, straw hat. Then she got closer and I could see her not classy gold lame sunglasses, her red nails which on first impression looked well put together but now close up they had designs on them and they were so pointy. The heavy earrings she wore were like testicles dangling from each ear.

It wasn't like I took a pill and then started having crazy and bizarre thoughts. I was having them all by myself. I keep starring in my own movies, I am also the producer and the director.

I thought it would be a good idea to go to a restaurant alone. I needed to get out. I sat in that damn corner for hours, maybe all day. It's a pretty corner as corners go. I never used to say words like 'daunting,' 'went missing,' 'tarmac,' 'broccoli rabe.' Really, where was broccoli rabe twenty years ago I never heard about it from my grandmother. But when it's cold I want those sweaters for my legs. Goodness me I have spent so much time trying to calm down and lick my wounds that I forgot to live, well I pretended I was living and in a way I was. I don't know what I want, but I want it now.

I got a portable laptop computer so it doesn't look like an office when I walk into my little place. The laptop is like a clam that opens during the day and closes up at night to sleep.

The cellphone they gave me. I talk to myself when I'm upset. Now I just pretend I'm on my cell phone so I look normal.

Sometimes I pray. One of the doctors told me to try that. I pretend that prayer works but really it only creates airwaves that ripple in concentric swerving lines into the universe and out farther than I can see. It doesn't help me. There is no linear way to help.

I love walking you never know what you are going to pass. Her cheap perfume smelled far worse than spoiled milk, I held my nose when we were yards from each other.

But it hurts. It hurts all the time. I have to do something. Oh the pain. Pain is an alarm signal. Extreme pain shuts you down but if pain is squelched your brain can think again. I take the medication but the side affects indicated possible death for which I am not ready.

I pick it up at the drugstore anyway, just to have it in case. Drugstores used to be bastions of safety and health, now they sell you products that make you sick so that you come back to get chemical pills to make you better.

All I know is I am older than I have ever been. I think that ATM machines should have panic buttons.

It's getting darker. I'm not sure how much longer I should walk around like this. I am wearing my lucky black outfit, the one with the stretchy pants and black long sleeve tee shirt with my hair in a ponytail.

I don't know why the stars look like they could fall from the sky. I daydream that they are really all seeds that watch us from way up there until we need to have something new grow and then it sends them down like sprinkles on ice cream.

I need to sit down. I walked into the coffee shop and ordered a fruit salad. Fruit is jewelry from the earth that you can eat. I hope nobody tries to start a conversation with me. It is getting cold in the north. I hope they decide to send for me to go to Florida with them.

A lady much older than me sat down at the next table. She stared at me. And then she said it.

"I used to be you. I was you." She looked at me, with longing from a far away time in her life, me with my lustrous hair and tan skin, so cute and sexy and warm. She had white straight hair and wrinkly tanned skin. "I was you," she said again so forlorn, as if she finally knew that she no longer had the time or the energy to try again.

Then she turned around and ordered her meal. Is that what I am going to look like years from now, and am I going to say strange things like that to strangers. She should only know who I am, then she wouldn't regret anything about her life or who knows, maybe her life was more exciting than mine. You know, you just can't tell anymore, I know that I look so normal.

Who is this sitting at the table to my right. He is so cute. He is just my type.

In my mind I pictured the way it would be. I would be my cutest. I would entice him with my wit and verbosity. He would invite me to his home. We would have a drink and have witty conversation.

My bill was paid, I had to leave the restaurant and go home, this was too much for me, I was too stressed, too tempted, I was like a cobra who had to dance to the music.

I got home and kept obsessing about him, as if the distance put anything of significance between us. I fell asleep in the reclining chair, with the television on, hoping to be able to change the subject. As I dozed off he was sitting next to me on the couch, wanting to move so much closer to me, so I let him. You are amazing, he would tell me. You are even more so, I would tell him as I slipped my pocketknife out of my pant elastic and pierced his heart as he peered into my eyes with such desire. The lights flickered, and then they went off.

It brings me such joy, murder with a smile.

HEADLINES

The newspapers know, the police know, the city knows. Serial Killer On The Loose. Moose loose, a moose on the loose. I am the moose. But only I know that, I'm sure of it. Who leaves a trail, why would a smart person like me leave a trail. They're calling them the black flower murders because of how the blood dries black in those beautiful floral designs.

WHEN REGA MET CARA

As I was laying on the spa table with stones all over my back covered with a warm herbal towel, I remembered the night I met him.

I was in more trouble than I had ever been. My bills were late, they were threatening to turn off my cable TV, my phone, electricity, stop all my credit cards. Other than that, I was feeling great. Go figure.

But I thought there's not enough time to procrastinate. I would like to be in love, I'll be the woman, he'll be the man, including he can support me because I am obviously not good at that anymore, not that I was ever spectacular at that, but I got by very fashionably and with much dignity.

I was just at that stage, bemoaning my woes, oh woe be me, I thought, as I had walked for hours around New York City, the world's largest outdoor mall that millions of people live in. Then I got an invitation.

I remember like it was yesterday. Ann and Arthur asked me to their dinner party. They said a friend of Arthur's from childhood would be there. I dressed my classiest, my richest. I arrived, and there was only Ann, Arthur and myself, for over an hour. What a waste of an outfit, I thought.

Then, just as I was finishing my first glass of

wine and my twentieth shrimp, the doorbell rang, Arthur answered it, and in he walked.

"Caranina, this is our friend Rega, Rega, this is Caranina." Arthur had to get out of the way because as Rega and I looked at each other a bolt of lightening flashed between us.

Now I had to watch what I eat and work out occasionally to look as good as I used to look naturally. As for him, now his belly hangs out over his pants just a tiny bit, but he is still a hunk and he knows it.

AMY SCREAMS

Cortland could not have imagined seeing Amy as an unstable person, vacillating between beautiful and nightmare, as if parts of her were disintegrating. And while of course Cortland knew all of this intellectually, the emotionality of his love and his guilt he knew sometimes could have an affect on him. He was, although he never liked to admit it, actually human. Dr. Olden assured him that this was temporary, a very normal response to the traumas she had been through. Just like soldiers lucky enough to leave the battlefield too often suffer terribly. Why would I expect more from her, other than that is what I wish, he thought. From every account she was strong and willful during her captivity. But now her tremors, her nightmares, her distrust, her screams and cries, the way her body becomes rigid when a door opens tells the truth.

She wants to live totally on her own again, but the doctors still say it is too soon and instead she'll often have an aide to help her, a woman who is trained to understand and guide her back into the real world that used to be kind to her, until she met me, he thought. Yes, he felt entirely responsible for this torturous experience she had, and vowed to always do everything in his power to make life right for her again.

The house was built by stonemasons of brick and river rock on a corner just a few blocks from the hospital.

For Heywood's sake, Cortland had again taken Samantha to lunch at her father's private club, to try to convince her to stay out of public places as gallery openings and dinner parties for awhile, but telling that to a young, intelligent vivacious lady is like telling a Mexican jumping bean to sit still.

When the phone rang and it was Heywood, he wasn't surprised. "Douglas, I'm glad to hear from you."

"I wish I knew how to tell you the reason for my call without losing my hold on all that I hold dear."

"What is it, Heywood. I can't imagine things getting more complex than they already are."

IF I DRESSED LIKE HER

I thought that if I dressed like her and tried to talk like her I could get away with it, but of course I still looked like me.

No matter how hard you try to change you're still you, or maybe with some people that's good but I would be much better off if I could start all over again.

My pony tail would give me away if you knew that is what you needed to look for, but who knows that. By the time a relevant person knows that he might not be able to express it so well any more.

CARA AND REGA IN FLORIDA

When I walk down the path of this South Florida hotel I see a menagerie of adorableness. The little lizards that zip down the path faster than a pea blown out of a straw, skinny black racer snakes that eat bugs, and there are bunny rabbits, turtles, squirrels that stop to lick their fingers in the middle of the street. At night so many frogs come out and just sit there like they're having a conference – until the headlights are almost on top of them.

Why does he have to love me so much. I know he does. We live in the best house, I have the most fabulous clothes, he makes sure everything is always perfect. But he's not hardly ever home, so what good is it.

He used to take me to Florida a few times a year, now finally we are here again after too long a time. I love to vacation here. But I need these walks away from him, I don't know what he's doing sometimes, he is secretive but today more so, he's not talking to me about it that's not new, but usually I can get a hint but I'm not getting a clue.

I just need to be there for him, that's what the magazines and the books always say, you have to be there for your man, be understanding, be gorgeous.

Oh but I need to be alone sometimes, so now

I'm in Florida with him what can I do. I can take little walks like I'm doing now. I can go shopping, I am the best shopper. I'll go to the Bal Harbor Shops they have everything I could ever want. I could go to the beach, the pool, I could get another massage on the roof with the hot stones, I could get my hair done but why bother I'd rather swim every day that I'm here and let my hair be wild, I'm never wild I always have to be so perfect for him but that's probably not even close to necessary because under his perfect veneer he is absolutely out of his mind and I am one of the few who really knows that.

Our private villa is always perfect. Everything is always perfect, doesn't it look like that.

Today I'm wearing a stunning halter top embroidered with silk flowers and birds with a long flowing skirt picking up the turquoise of the bird feathers. Just like all the pools here. When I go to the pool they are playing rumba music, like they have for decades, it feels so festive.

But why do I think something is happening that's different. Because he had Paul meet us down here. Ever since I heard that his aide Paul was going to be here I knew there was something unusual. Rega likes to be with the boys. He's one of those men who feels the most manly showing off to other men to show how powerful and smart he is.

Some of my friends tell me that their husbands admit certain things to them, like that they are frightened sometimes, don't feel so capable sometimes. But not my Rega. He never lets anyone think he is anything less than incredible.

I'm just a few blocks from the villa now. He won't like it if he knows I walked out of the property alone without a guard. Who knows, maybe they've been watching me all along.

If I had wanted a normal relationship I would not have picked him. I knew from the start that he was different, he had that edge, that excitement, and I wanted that in my world. Why I wanted that I don't really know but when I was younger it seemed so important.

It's only three in the afternoon. We had our morning coffee together on our private veranda facing the ocean but on a second level so no one could just walk in from the beach. Levels, he always likes levels, says he could hide better if there are levels, so our house at home in the North has four stories, who lives in a house with four stories.

"My Cara, Cara there you are," I heard his voice coming from down and around the path leading from the hotel lobby to the pool. He looked so happy to see me I thought something wonderful was going on. He even ran over to me and hugged me, I promise this never happens.

"Hello my handsome man," I say in return, the tropics always make conversation flow more breezily.

"Cara, I've been worried about you, you didn't tell me you were going for a walk. I got off the phone and you were gone. Nobody saw you leave! You didn't even leave a note. I was so worried."

How cute was this tough man. After all these years I swear I've never seen him quite like this.

"Nothing, nothing to worry about my darling. Really, I walked a little around the grounds and just kept walking, it wasn't a plan." Or was it, I thought to myself.

I need to understand him cause he's my guy. I need to know what's going on cause my life and my future are at stake. I know I'm covered, but I don't want to be surprised, although I am always constantly surprised by him.

Oh no, this isn't good, I sound like a swooning girl in a romance novel, and that's not what this is. This is really the wild wild west in gorgeous designer clothes.

GET OUT FRANK

She moved around her bed, but things didn't feel right. She didn't know why but her head was spinning and all she wanted to do was go back to sleep but someone was knocking on the door and for a moment she thought the noise was a dream but the insistent banging was waking her up. She opened her eyes, she wasn't home in her own room. Rega wasn't there. Then she heard him talking to someone in the living room.

"You idiot," Rega groused as he opened the front door. "What the hell are you doing here." He stepped back from the door and then in an instant pulled the man into the room.

"I'm only here to protect you, you know that."

"Protect me from what," Rega protested, trying hard not to scream. "I'm on fuckin vacation with my wife!"

"We're supposed to report to you when we get a bite. They had us in this underground place for a coupla days, just an hour or so from here. They tied us up, they left me in solitary, they questioned us. And then they took us somewhere and just let us go. It was crazy."

"How the hell did you know where to find me?"

"All the guys know where you always are Mr. Rega, sir."

All Rega could think of was how much trouble Frank kept causing. He had to get rid of him, he should have fired him after his insanity with that girl.

"Listen, Frank. I want you to leave here right now and forget you ever saw me. I want you to get in touch with Jimmy and tell him everything. I'm seeing him later for a meeting. Don't ever come around near me again or you'll get us all into more trouble than you could ever dream of."

"But sir..."

"I know you wanted to be the big shot and talk to me, but that's not happening today, here, right now. Now go, do what I said, get outta here." And with that Rega steered him out of the room, shut the door and vowed to ax him when he got back up north.

SAMANTHA IN CANNES

"What are you crazy Heywood? This is the worst time to think of traveling, you could not be more vulnerable and you know that. Don't you think they're waiting for you to make that kind of a move?"

"Look Cortland," Heywood responded. "I know everyone is doing everything they can to find this threat, of course I know that. And I have thus far taken every precaution both for myself and for my family. But Samantha is young, she can't take this isolation. As a matter of fact I have never seen her so unhappy in recent years."

"Okay Heywood, my friend. I'm at least willing to listen. What is it that you are proposing?"

"I want to take Samantha away, even if it is for just a few days," Heywood said with a voice less sure of itself than usual. "I am supposed to be one of the most objective thinkers in the world, but my heart melts when my daughter wants anything at all."

"Well, what exactly do you want to do?"

"I want to take her to Europe for a few days."

"To Europe? You don't think word will get out? You don't think you'll be followed? You think an international trip won't put a spotlight right on you?"

"I know my daughter. This is what would make her happy. Her favorite spot on the planet is the South of France, Cannes. She just loves it there. I would do anything to raise her spirits and I know that would."

Heywood and Samantha were on a secured flight the next night, with passports and documentation that would stymie the best intels. The only stipulation was that Samantha was to wear her hair up and under a hat at all times, which she happily made into an enjoyable challenge. And Heywood agreed to wear a fedora and uncharacteristic sunglasses, for which he chose gold rimmed Porsche Carrera.

"Father, thank you for this," Samantha said as she hugged the man she respected more than any other in the world. "I feel totally spoiled, as usual, and I know that this time you have put an investigation, and possibly our lives, in jeopardy just to make me happy." Then she hesitated and added, "You could have said no to me. Why didn't you this time?"

"The truth is my Sammy, I too was getting bored sitting in the house for all of these months. And then you had been traveling for such a long time, I thought it would be a treasure for us to have this kind of special time together. Also, the timing is perfect, your mother has her museum luncheons this week, and she thought this would be nice for us as long as we are careful, which she knows we will be."

They walked on the Croisette, the street that bordered the perimeter of the Mediterranean Sea on one side, a two way street with a flower and palm tree island in the middle. Old European hotels, with the maritime alps cuddling behind them line the other side, all with magnificent views. They walked past the Carlton, where they usually stayed. But since they were trying to be just a little low key, they stayed instead around the corner at the Croisette Beach, a lovely boutique hotel that served an exquisite breakfast in the room.

"There is no coffee like this in the whole wide world," Samantha would say at each breakfast in the living room of the suite as she savored the croissants that melted in her mouth.

They had one of the penthouses with spectacular views of the alps and the sea, above a quaint narrow street bordered by cement flower pots.

They walked past prestigious shops and hotels as Chanel, Ralph Lauren, Hotel Gray d'Albion, The Martinez until they saw the all too modern Palais where the Cannes Film Festival, and the MIDEM international music conferences, were held each year. Heywood had loved the original Palais, the building was still there of course, several blocks away and across the street, with its traditional architecture. But he understood, or at least tried to, that modern times and increasing populations required these modern enormous structures even in their beloved Cannes, but it never looked right to him, never blended in well enough. And behind and along side it were yachts, dozens of magnificent yachts, probably some of his friends were in town.

Ah the Mediterranean sea air here is like no other, Heywood thought as he breathed deeply, ever amazed at the astounding expanse of countries and history on the other sides of this sea.

They turned right up the hill, where the roads were no wider than a 1950's Cadillac, and walked past little shops, apartments, with the purr of French vowels lulling past them as they walked towards one of their favorite restaurants in the village, La Mere Besson.

"*Mais oui, papa, oh merci,*" Samantha said as they took their seats. "Now I know that we are really here."

Heywood would never deprive his daughter of anything. She was as bright as he, and he was hoping that she would get involved in her own brand of government related work.

They had a sumptuous meal, shopped with their untraceable cards, and walked down the hill to the Carlton lobby for an afternoon coffee and sweet. Oh how it used to be here years ago, he recalled, when he would see world luminaries behaving nonchalantly.

Samantha left for the ladies room, one of her favorites in a commercial establishment with the wood, marble, brass, and mirrors and the individual cozy little toilet rooms with the cleverly self-changing seat covers.

It was here, Heywood remembered, that he and Lyla had conceived Samantha those years ago, and here she was, almost a woman, and he was delighted to indulge her. He had to make sure that she would be ready to take on enormous new responsibilities when they returned. She was going to be offered a position in this organization, an expertise she was raised knowing like most children hear their ABCs.

SHE KNOWS TONY CAMERA

She had to work on what she would say to him if they could have a private conversation. You've got something I need. And I have something you need.

But first let me explain myself. I can't help it. What it does for me, makes me feel important, I know I can attract them. Men ogle over me, sometimes there is pleasure the normal way, sometimes that's so boring, one day I flipped over a line and since then I do other things, and there is no flipping back.

I needed to expand my repertoire. Then everything after that is predictable, boring.

But I guess you're lucky, you only got to see my debutante side. When we were younger you promised to protect me but you didn't. So I had to find you, to be near you, that was the only way I could ever feel safe. You never knew it was me, but that's okay, I was always safe near you.

Bet you thought only men could be crazy. Even though you're in love with her, I saw you looking at me one day. That look, you know, when a man is interested. I saw you look at my body, you knew I had the power. I know that. All I have to say to a guy is let's go out, hint that he could have some, and boom, the rest is whatever fun I want it to be with the added genius of my carvings.

I could tell him that I grew up with Tony Camera. But not yet.

But why, you would ask. Would she ever get the chance to tell him. I think he would respect me so much more when he finds out that it's not only that I am in his world. It's that he might be the biggest hunted animal on the planet right now, I know that, but I'm the biggest unsolved mystery in the world right now. Did he ever have headlines like mine? And anyway, I know his real name.

AMY RUNS TO THE OCEAN

She had asked Cortland to take her to Jones Beach on Long Island at 6:30 a.m. before the crowds, and he did that for her. Maybe because this is where they met. This mattered for every reason. But this time she just needed that air, that ability to look forever in the distance without buildings or trees, just ocean and sky.

After they put the towel down she told Cortland that she wanted to feel the sand on her toes, so she took off her sneakers and socks.

As soon as her feet touched the sand she ran, she ran like there was the force of every moment of her life under her feet, propelling every toe to sing through the air with a feeling of peace and freedom that she was sure she had felt before but it was so very long ago.

She was running from, she was running to, everything was going to be okay now. The sky was blue, the sand was soft, the air was filled with salt and dew and little breezes.

She knew that she was here now, that this is where she always had to be – in this mood, in this knowing, in this certainty of it all.

It was like Footsteps, the poem that made her cry every time, even right now her tears were wetter than the ocean, deeper than the soul.

She watched the waves reach the dry sand, only to pull it towards itself leaving the surface sparkling with water bubbles of the breath of tiny creatures digging their way.

I knew that I had to run faster than ever before. It was the only way to unglue from the past and fly to the next place. I did not want to look behind me. The point was there, over there, far far over there where the beams of sunshine tickled the water splashing onto the sand and the grass and the seaweed that had rolled to here and there.

I lay at the edge where I was at one with the air and the sand and the water lapping in while my long hair cascaded behind me, my scalp felt the rushes of salty ocean and warm clean air whooshing over my entire body.

SAMANTHA'S BOYFRIEND

I was on The Promenade de la Croisette – in Cannes, *oui, c'est le French Riviera, my favorite place.* Why would I want to be anyplace else.

I had flown into the Nice Côte d'Azur Airport almost a year before life had become frightening and limiting. I had checked into the Carlton Hotel, where Heywood was also staying, showered, took a nap and then stepped out onto the terrace and savored the view of the Mediterranean Sea. This is perfection, I had thought, I can breath again, every part of me feels better here. On the third day Heywood had meetings later in town and wanted to first take a nap in his suite so I took a long walk on my favorite street with stops in shops that I missed so much. I made lunch plans with old friends.

It was our first meeting, now always a memory living somewhere in the arc of the rainbow way up high. It was a moment, a knowing, a certainty awash in glow forever.

I remember immediately how I thought that no cuff ever sat on a wrist as yours did, no eyes were as contentedly joyful, no hand felt so warm.

Before lunch I had shopped and bought a new outfit, pocketbook and shoes, all would be messengered to the hotel. I only had to walk a block back to the Carlton where we were to have lunch, drinks first in the lobby, with a group of friends I had no idea till you sat down in our little grouping that you would be among them.

Am I obsessed with Cannes, yes, can I help but always refer to it any chance I can, no I will always do that. Other than that I can control myself quite well.

I was calmly obsessed about you. I couldn't stop turning my head to look at you, as reserved as I was trying to be and as delighted as I was to see my dear friends Ardsley and Carrie Bard, Carmella Parrington and Selma Katzen.

They introduced us – we reached across air that had never been touched before, immediately a sizzle between us amid a field of swirling lights. Our hands knew the other was moving towards each other, and then finally we shook hands and you didn't let go for the longest time. I thought we were going to float away and have our own conversation perched just under the stars with the sea twinkling below.

You grew up differently but compatibly it seemed. Your family had government involvement, they were also in trade, making enormous worldwide deals. But what were they trading. You swore it wasn't arms or drugs. Products like exceptional cars, luxury goods, gold, fine watches, art. I thought what an interesting assemblage.

If your family met my family, I felt certain that all would be fine and right. Surely they already knew of one another, but had never met in that rarefied world of sophisticated international relations.

I know my father so well. Heywood earned his position simply because there was no other person more suited to navigate the world stage than he. He was constantly impressive. He could be intimidating.

Your name is Andre Jardin – I had even allowed myself to think how nice our names joined would sound, I admit I wrote it once to see what the signature would look like. But I am so much more mature than that, so I never did it again.

Your eyes were blue, I wished they weren't

sometimes they were so hard to look into they were so disarmingly soothing. It was like everything about you showered me with rays of tenderness, all new feelings. You were so earnest, handsome and adorable.

We were both from the North Shore of Long Island. I was from Roslyn, you were from Great Neck – similar but different.

I used to know Great Neck perfectly well; my grandmother on my mother's side lived there in a grand house in Kings Point with several acres of land so from the age of five I was the little world explorer on what felt like a universe when I visited there. Everything there seemed magical – my grandfather had peach and pear trees planted and they grew there, we could eat the fruit, I remember thinking that was amazing.

We used to all go out to dinner where there were popovers, puffy empty centered freshly baked rolls delivered in baskets at Patricia Murphy's.

Where are you now. We were in the South of France together so often for almost a year while I attended classes and you were on assignments for your father. Both of our fathers are power men in the world.

We met again at a café on a Sunday morning, I with a cup of coffee and a brioche, you with champagne. That was our turning point.

AMY REMEMBERS CORTLAND

Wait a minute, I'm dying here and that's not how I want to live.

It was like a bubble burst in my head and gravity carried my hand to the phone while, at the same time, a long ignored miniature file folder in my brain manipulated my fingers to dial a certain number.

As soon as I heard Cortland's voice I felt a warmth creep over me and through me that I hadn't felt in so long. For the first time since I had been kidnapped, after all of his visits to me in the hospital, all of the walks we took around the grounds, as he talked and pointed out the beautiful gifts of nature, as I walked with him, hardly touching, not holding hands, me not saying a word. Our night out to dinner and dancing had begun to reignite some things about us. And now, on the phone, I couldn't stop talking. We were on the phone for over two hours. I had forgotten what it was like to really want to talk to somebody.

So many of my memories were a blur. I had so many questions. I knew that I did not have a handle on exactly how long I had been captive.

Snippets of my recollections had been coming back while I was working out in the hospital gym, especially when they had me work with personal trainers, which at first I feared with every fiber in me – but they were kind, they used a purposefully limited tactile connection combined with some calmly expressed encouraging instructions so I could no longer just travel around my own thoughts. But I mostly liked the group classes, each aerobics session had it's own personality, it's own music, it's own energy, it's own beat. I loved the energy of the group classes, it made me feel like I was soaring. Some of the instructors had great taste in music, set the speed just right, and moving to it was utter and pure joy. Usually I was simply at one with the dance at hand. And at some point I started to break through. That freedom, that movement rearranged my body, my mood, the details of all the cobwebs I had been stuck with were disintegrating.

CORTLAND VISITS GRETA

Cortland drove through the forest until he got to the road only few knew lead to the headquarters of GRETA where meetings could comfortably be held. Only a select few knew that GRETA existed. Even before Nixon subverted the decency of democracy, in retrospect now from the constant subversion we are experiencing, it was then in such limited ways, but it was indeed then that it was determined that there needed to be a watchful eye, not controlled or directly connected to the government, that could monitor every person and event in the administration of our country so that there could never be a successful misuse of power in the United States again.

Keeping track of the world's military capacities and every nation's intentions had been formidable enough. But when it is realized that individuals and corporations can master the same strengths, the questions, including how do you watch over a hundred million possibilities, become exactly what you must be capable of doing every second of every day.

You need to start with one good spy in every possible situation to know anything at all. That is where the singular members of GRETA came from, that is the air they breathe.

Cortland parked his car and started to walk towards GRETA headquarters when Garrison came out and said, "Today we take a drive, my friend."

CORTLAND WITH GARRISON

"If we're so smart why haven't we solved this already," Cortland asked as he drove with Garrison towards upstate New York. They were going to a location that, years ago, had been a secret government installation built into a mountain.

"Of course I speak to Heywood just about every day, and of course he is worried far more about Samantha than about himself. He took her to France, just to get away for a few days, for himself, but mostly for her, and now he's found out that she met someone new, she has a boyfriend."

"Where did she meet him?" Garrison asked.

"In France. When she was there last year. She was introduced by friends, usually the best and safest way, so presumably she has his provenance from trusted sources."

"When did it become serious?"

"Those details we don't have yet. Heywood thought it odd that she hadn't mentioned him before, while it seems that she has known him for months. Evidently something new happened between them only recently."

They had driven off the main road some time ago, wandering down back roads, it seemed.

"There it is," Garrison said.

"There what is?" Cortland asked.

"Our secret mountain. We always need to have a back-up place and a back-up plan. I've been wanting to show this to you."

"What took you so long?"

"Most everything according to immediate need. If in fact the threat to Heywood is real and serious, we can bring him and his family here for as long as needs be. Nobody would ever find them here."

Cortland looked around, left, right, up, down. "I don't see anything but the rocky side of a mountain, trees, grass, bushes, plants, sky."

He noticed Garrison pushing buttons on his wrist watch and the rock side of the mountain opened up just enough for the car to drive through, and immediately closed behind them.

"Garrison, I have been doing this for several decades, I was sure nothing could ever surprise me again, but this certainly did. Where in the hell are we."

They got out of the car, as if they were on an underground country road. There were entrances to homes on either side of the street. They went into one.

"This is where they would stay. There would be guards if we had to bring them here."

Cortland saw that there was a living room, sleeping quarters, kitchen. All ready to be occupied. One of the buildings that looked like a country home was actually an office with guards around the clock.

ANGRY ALL THE TIME

I don't know what it is. I'm just angry all the time. What is that called, does it have a name.

I'll get dressed, after that I won't have much to think about. Think think think. I don't want to think so much anymore. It wears you down, it really does, all those thoughts.

Maybe I'll travel with Mr. Rega's boys. Oh so many of them, I wonder which one will want to be first. Mr. Rega is always so impressed with my work, he always was, if he only knew what I really do.

Who knows the house better than me, about those hidden hallways and stairs, it's a crazy maze with secret sliding walls like in the movies.

If I go to Florida to meet them, maybe they'll need my help with something. But she hadn't invited me. But maybe it will clear my head. I've been too busy. What a schedule, I don't want a schedule I just want to do what I feel like doing.

HEYWOOD TELLS CORTLAND

If Cortland didn't know where she was every second of every day, he thought, then maybe he was losing that special touch he always had for the hardest most specialized and complex projects. Amy could not be located this entire afternoon, not by the house staff, not by her guards. He had SOSs everywhere, how could she just have wandered off, why would she do this after all that has gone on.

As he was trying to figure out where she was, his secure cell phone rang, temporarily taking him out of his dread.

"Cortland here."

"Cortland, it's me, Heywood. We have to talk. Something new has happened and I don't know whether to be thrilled or worried."

"Well, let's not panic just yet Heywood. What in the world is going on."

"It's my Samantha. As you well know, she had the most wonderful trip to Europe, but she has been totally miserable since she's returned as we have had to keep her home and away from all of her friends and activities because of the threats to me. Of course except for those few days in France and a few gallery openings. But today there was new information. You know me for a long time, Cortland, and you know that I don't surprise easily. But my Samantha has me drained and a wreck."

"What in the world is it Heywood. Do you want to tell me now, on the phone, or do you want me to stop by. I'm only about a half hour from your house."

"Well then come by, yes, I think you should. I'm afraid that this could be deeper than even my Samantha could ever imagine." He paused, then continued, "Cortland, she has met someone, I don't know him, I've not vetted him. What if it is someone who dazzled her and she fell for it but he is really someone who we would all want to avoid. I am frantic over this."

Now Cortland understood. Especially now, any unknowns feel menacing. But what an awful way for them to try to get to Heywood, and how brilliant, and a version of what he has always feared the most – using his daughter to get to him.

"It must have been hard for her to tell you about this, Heywood. What information did she give you about him? She is very bright, we know that. I can't imagine that she would fall for someone who was not absolutely substantial."

"She has only told me that he is handsome, well read, went to the best universities, he's from a good family, and he has enough money to support her for the rest of her life, if that is what she wants...." His voice got lower the more he spoke, and then he just hesitated.

"What is it Heywood. This sounds like every father's dream. The daughter meets someone special, someone who makes her happy."

"I can't figure out why she didn't mention him in a special way before. She told us that she met wonderful people in her travels, that she has terrific new friends, that she had a few dates but nothing special. Nothing special made her fall in love?"

"I'll be there soon. Don't worry. We will know everything we need to know about him in just a few hours. Can Samantha join us after a short time during our meeting? I'm sure that I will want to ask her questions."

"Yes, of course, she will be there. See you then."

By the time they finished their conversation, Andre Jardin's name was being investigated in every global database.

FLORIDA LIMELIGHT

In the outskirts of Palm Beach there was a bar called the Limelight where later that day some of Rega's Florida friends held court in the privacy of the back room.

"I figured it was about a hundred miles from here. That's all I know. They had us blindfolded the whole time, so how was I supposed to really know where I was."

"Well, Frank, let's figure that was the point, heh?" Vinnie was always in control of himself, he felt so self-contained, and knew he was probably always the wisest one in the room. But Frank, he could get us all into trouble, he always had to do too much, try too hard.

WE DIDN'T GET ALONG

We didn't get along at all. We were like oil and water, dipped in cliché. He hated what I wore on the plane. I could see his face deflate, although not his stomach, when I deplaned. He said we don't wear shoes like those here. It was over before it had begun. But I was determined that we could still make it a special ten days, even if we mostly ignored each other.

From then on we were up against each other at every pass, no insult was left unhurled, no nasty look out the corner of our eyes, in disbelief of some behavior, went unscorned.

He was exactly how he had been in first grade. He had had a crush on me since I was five years old. He had pretended on the phone that he had a sense of humor. We laughed so much. He thought he was being elitist, but he was simply not living. Where there could have been so much joy, there was a bizarre negativity. And without my having anything at all to do with it, in a year he was gone.

But I had some plastic surgery since then.

EGGSHELLS

If you keep stepping on eggshells, you're never really walking.

I had to pee, the bathroom on the plane is so small. If I wear a wig, they won't know it's me.

I rolled up five strips of toilet paper to clean the seat just in case someone before me dripped. And there is just about nothing more horrible than sitting on a stranger's drips. Then I used up three long strips of toilet paper to cover the seat before I sat.

I ordered the cloud formations this afternoon, ladies and gentlemen. Look out your airplane window now. Today we have blue sky with white fluffy cotton ball mountains. Once I was on the airplane and cozy in my seat I fell asleep. I dreamt that a snake crawled up the side of the storage room door, it was black and thin, about two feet long. Why did I dream that maybe because I slithered so gracefully past the crowds in the airport, but once upon a time I dreamt of a prince on a white horse, that was a better dream.

I had to go to the bathroom in the airport too. Every time I open a stall in a public bathroom I open the door slowly. I don't know how to explain it, but I am always sure that I will see a dead body slumped on the toilet seat, and I am practically peeing in my pants already who could hold it in anymore what an inconvenience that would be.

Finally we landed. I was seated in the first row of lowly coach class, and out the window was a young man directing the plane towards the gate. From my seat I could see pieces of gold jewelry reflecting the sun sparkling from his nose. In the distance I can see a suspension bridge, with cars racing over it, with rays of sunshine bouncing off their chrome. And airplanes taxiing lazily to position. All huge capsules moving people. Moving me to my next adventures.

COLTER AND GRANGE CLUES

They sat in Colter's ever beige office, eating their usual any kind of beef sandwiches. The only thing new Colter had gotten for his office in the last decade was the set of black and beige striped fabric arm chairs, one on either side of the beige couch, with the coffee table in the middle holding the candy wrappers and coffee mugs. Nice looking office for some really horrible situations.

They had clippings from every crime that had the signature My Name Is Rita on it. There were fifteen, that they knew about, in New York, three in the South of France and a few in South Florida.

Astonishingly, there were no real clues yet. How was that possible.

The lipstick used to write My Name Is Rita is a Revlon shade of red that had been around for over twenty years. There were always microscopically slight variations based on date and location of manufacture and sale. Tests showed that the lipsticks were manufactured in New Jersey, purchased in New York, Connecticut, France and Florida between the 1960's and into the 2000's. Well, that was something.

CENTRAL PARK

In Central Park, a day in March, the temperature is in the low 60's. They're hiking, walking, roller blading, babies are crying in rows of nannies with blue strollers.

How will I explain that I heard about him, through the walls. Sometimes men talk so loud. They obviously never imagined that anyone would be listening.

"He is leaving no stone, no pebble, no rock, no boulder unturned. He and whoever else were hired."

"How'd you get his name?"

And then he explained how they made Sal, Vinnie, Lou and Frank disappear and have some memory loss when they took them to some secret place. They were beaten and demeaned while weird music played on some kind of system that made them vibrate to it.

The park is jammed, good, because park acquisitions are successful. I hear a boyfriend scream to his girlfriend, "you have bubbly vagina sulfa farts." I can never tell this to anyone. I thought I had issues.

Suddenly the sun broke through, the bulbing flowers haven't popped, not yet, it's too soon, I'm getting itchy, I've got the heebie geebies.

How long can I keep this up, my employers depend on me. But I see someone really cute over there.

THE BUS

The first bus broke down on the other side of the Midtown Tunnel, which meant that the twenty-five passengers from that bus were about to be loaded on to mine. *Quel* drag.

I already had my black purse and my black leather overnight bag on the seat next to me. Oh, I had so looked forward to sitting alone and not feeling squished. I wanted to think, write, enjoy the solitude as different from the rush and zippy energy of the last months. I practically held my breath as the new passengers filed down the narrow aisle, with their travel bags and the young ones with their back packs bumping and rubbing against my arm, banging against my shoulder I wanted to punch them all.

After a few minutes I breathed relief while feeling the ire of the sweet older lady sitting diagonally behind me who was being crushed by the woman next to her. We had just made neighborly comments, now she was pissed, however genteelly.

White Castle, Rego Park, Queens Boulevard, I need new territory, new blood, new pickins. Why does the bus have to stop right by the cemetery. It used to be quaint here, the candy store on the corner, the yoyo's, black and white sodas, Spalding balls and how they smelled when they were new.

Is there an actual funeral, does anyone recover from our little rendezvous or are my designs simply too profound.

Where do they bring my works of art, I've always pondered. After they wonder at my designs. I'm sure that they take pictures for their proof and their archives. Is there a book, there should be a book called Designs By Rita. Oh I would be so proud.

Now it's dark. I'm finished what I set out to do. You'll read about it soon I'm sure.

WHY DIDN'T I TELL THEM

I'm finally starting to feel like myself again after spending just a few days in Florida. I've been so normal for such a long time, weeks I think, I am satisfied that I have turned the corner from the deepest insanity to the best I will ever be. Why didn't I tell them that I've been through this before. You just can't go faster than the car in front of you. I'm stressed all the time, can you blame me. But that's not what's on my mind. What is on my mind is the fact that everything keeps changing, and I mean everything. One minute I'm out of my mind, and now I'm just taking a walk like anyone else.

I wondered if I had died already and where I was, where you went. I had this thought while driving down Hagen Ranch Road in Boynton Beach, Florida past the community of houses that had one garage for your car and another for your plane, while the road that went straight through it was the runway. Things like that help you figure out if you are dead or alive, because who could make up that kind of a set up.

I was going to the beach that day because it was another beautiful tropical day. The only thing that wasn't okay was what I was going to do later. What is the matter with me, why can't I have the same kind of fun as everyone else. I am just so unique.

SLEEPING

He is sleeping in the next room, I can hear him snoring, I can tell he's resting on the reclining green leather chair that has gorgeous brass decorative brass tacks the domed heads which are the size of a dime.

Finally I was alone, if only for a few minutes. I don't like to be watched all the time, asked what I'm doing all the time, not allowed to have some time to myself.

I know I need watching over sometimes, my transition back into the world is not easy. I suffer from depression, flashbacks, sadness, guilt, and heavy duty PTSD.

It could be a simple request – and I freak, I feel like I'm being forced and coerced to agree to something that I do not agree with and I am terrified, shaking, sweating, furious, heartbroken.

I had already decided on something, please stop trying to change my mind.

THE CAVE WAS COLD

The cave was cold. Four times a year the inside air temperature was lowered to its minimal for proper maintenance of the facility. Everyone dressed warmly to not drastically affect the running of every day life there. The only areas where the temperature never changed were the labs and where fresh vegetables, herbs and fruits were grown, salmon and shrimp were spawned and fresh water was in constant circulation. They needed to be as self sufficient as possible.

HIS HANDWRITING

I had started again to save everything that had his handwriting on it, because I still felt the loss of having thrown all of that away so many years ago as if throwing all those things away would really remove him from my life.

SECRET NY APARTMENT

Whenever I can I stop in New York City and stay a day or more in my secret apartment that I try not to tell anyone about, a really nice doorman building with a driveway in a beautiful neighborhood always walking distance to Central Park.

In this city there's a different kind of air, buzz, attitude, a different kind of walking. Your sneakers take you on three hour walks from Greenwich Village to the Upper East Side and it is exhilarating.

My favorite thing to eat when I'm in my New York apartment is an avocado. I like to cut it in half, take a spoon and eat the green custard right from the shell like it was chocolate pudding.

Sometimes I would rather be in Florida in the constant warm no coat or boots. You drive you never ruin your heels by grating them on the cement sidewalks or mush them in the oil slicked, doggie doody urined streets. Always something unexpected happens in NY, which can ruin plans, but then always something else materializes as if out of nowhere.

WALKING ON BARROW

Maybe it's all over for me, I thought. Is this how it's going to end? I'll be a little teeny paragraph on the bottom of a page in the *New York Post* saying girl found beaten, raped and dead in the Village. I was walking down one of those quaint Greenwich Village streets, it was only about ten o'clock on a Friday night in October, it was cool but not cold, people were strolling except on the block that I was walking on. There was no one.

It was a street of charming townhouses with little gates between them, and old red brick low-rise apartment buildings. I only had one block to go before I turned left, walked past a few buildings and I'd be home. I saw a young man across the street walking in my direction. He was dressed Ivy League, off white cotton jacket over a plaid shirt, and nice looking tan slacks. Amazing what you can notice.

Then all of a sudden he was walking diagonally across the street right to me. What? He grabbed my arm and said, "I have a knife and if you don't do what I say I'm going to cut up your pretty little face."

Well, this is different, I thought. What the hell do I do now. Of course I decided to simply act calm and rational and figure whatever this was would be over in a few minutes. I asked him, "What do you want?" He said, "Give me all your money."

My luck, I hadn't gone to the cash machine that day, I didn't have but a few dollars and some change in my wallet. I was wearing slacks, a sweater and a short mink jacket with a really beautiful brown striped lining. When I told him that I didn't have hardly any money, maybe just a few dollars, he looked at me like I was crazy and grabbed for my solid gold necklace that I wore all the time because it had been my grandfather's watch chain and the clasp was soldered shut and he ripped it off my neck.

Then he had another idea. Before I realized what was happening, he took my hands, snatched them apart and quickly sneaked his fingers under and up my sweater.

That's when I went into action because I remembered an article in a lady's magazine that I had just recently read. A man had broken into her apartment and was about to attack her. The woman thought to herself this man is trying to hurt me, he's bigger than I am, he's stronger that I am, what can I do, what do I have, how can I save myself. All she had, she realized, was her gift of gab. So after that epiphany, I hardly shut up.

I pulled his hand out from under my sweater and told him that the reason my breasts were so small, for which I had never been so grateful, was that I had a terrible disgusting contagious disease. I made up a long awful sounding medical word, and told him that they had to be cut off, and if he touched my skin anywhere near them he could catch it. I said I just got out of the hospital from it. I was trying to make him nauseous of me, I thought that if I made him sick he wouldn't want to touch me and he would leave me alone.

He hurled me against cars parked just next to us, and then he tried to get me off the street and into a deserted building entrance, but all the doors were locked so he couldn't get in. Then he dragged me by the arm and slammed me into a fence between two townhouses so that he could rape me there but it was locked shut. He told me that he had a gun and that if

I tried anything he was ready to use it. I was sniveling by then, and tried to appeal to his emotions, I asked him if he had a sister, and could he imagine something like this happening to his sister, because I figured that if he had a sister and realized that I was somebody's sister he would stop frightening me. But he didn't care, he kept pulling me down the street.

All the while I thought of running, I thought of screaming. I wondered whether or not he actually had a weapon, but should I take a chance, what should I do. I looked around me. Everything was the same as any other time I've walked on this street except that now it was a backdrop for a horror movie that I was starring in.

He's pulling me down the street, he's looking for an opening between buildings so he could get me off the sidewalk. I'm whimpering and I really couldn't stand it any more so I told him that he was making me so nervous I was having diarrhea, I figured who would want to rape someone who was having diarrhea, and all of a sudden he tossed me away and said if I ever tell anyone about this he will find me again and then he was gone.

I hadn't realized how dark it was, but I was alive, and all I could think of was something my mother told me when I was young, and that is, if you think someone is following you don't go home because if you do the bad guys will know where you live. So instead of turning onto my street I walked to the next street, looking around me every second. I was shaking but determined as I was sure he was hiding somewhere nearby ready to leap out and start all over with me and worse, far worse.

Finally there was cab. I hailed it, I got in, all of the tension from the utter fear poured out and I started to cry hysterically. I sobbed telling the taxi driver that I had just been mugged, practically raped and killed, that I didn't have any money with me because I had to give it to the man who hurt me, but when we get to my friend's apartment house he would have money so don't worry. The taxi driver immediately sped the car to the curb, slammed on the brakes, raised his voice and said to me, "lady, you don't have money get out of my taxi."

I couldn't process this. How could he do this to a girl who said she just got mugged. But then I realized he probably thought I was a drug addict with my dark brown eye make-up dripping down my face and I'm crying uncontrollably. I looked at his license with his picture that was in a clear plastic holder on the back of his seat and I saw that his last name was Clark, so I said to him between sniffles, "Mr. Clark, I'm a nice girl from Long Island, I went to school, everybody loves me. I am telling you that this is what happened to me tonight and you are telling me to get out of your taxi. That man could still be here watching for me!!!" And he screamed, "get out!"

We had driven exactly half a block, stopped at the red light most of the time. I got out of his car, thought my life is over now, he's got to be hovering around still, I'm finished, I'm dead. But then came another taxi and I didn't say a word, turns out that between the quarters, nickels and dimes at the bottom of my bag I had just enough to pay for the ride to Stanley's.

Thank goodness Stanley was home, I took a chance, there were no cell phones yet. Stanley was shocked by my story, and took me right away to the local police station. They drove us up and down every street in the neighborhood hoping we'd see him walking around but nothing. Then back to the police station they showed me mug shots. Nothing. That was it, it was over. That night I slept on Stanley's couch. He's lucky we're such good friends.

MEETING FOR DRINKS

You mother fucker, you wonderful gorgeous handsome mother fucker. I thought we were having dinner tonight but no, we were just meeting for drinks and then you went on to your other plans. Well guess what, I have other plans too. It's not that hard to put a few plans together, so I did just that.

There are plans and there are plans I said clicheyedly, and if I want to clichey well then I certainly will and without your goddamn permission who in the hell do you think you are.

You found a girlfriend, I am going to find myself a boyfriend. Everyone wants me, I know that, but only a few people can actually have me to any degree at all emotionally, intellectually, spiritually, sexually. I'm very picky. But that's besides the point, isn't it, isn't it really all about class. You either have class or you don't. You could have money or not, closets full of clothes or not, gorgeous hair or not, but you either have class or you don't. I have class and I know that.

So, what am I going to do with all that class. Hmmm, let's see. I can take a walk in the park, it's pretty early so it's not dark yet, or I can pack a few things and take a plane to Nice, France and then taxi to Cannes. Yes, I think that is what I am in the mood to do.

I heard you were looking for me, although you won't know it's me, I have deep cover.

I need to walk on the Croisette, sit in the lobby of the Carlton and have a glass of milk with a side of chocolate ice cream, spoon some ice cream in the milk and boom, that is the only way you can have a glass of chocolate milk in the Carlton lobby. I love that lobby. I love the ladies room, the old world wooden doors, the marble, the private sitting rooms. The toilet that keeps covering itself with fresh paper. Every woman who goes there loves that ladies' room.

But I won't go to France now, I really can't, I have to stay in town, I need to be here. I have to wait till I have actual vacation time. I heard that old friends might be there. Why, that was a thought that kept me up at night. Should I wash off my make-up while I'm having these thoughts or maybe I'll go out for a walk in a while, no I won't do that it's raining. I'll walk in the morning.

What would I do if I saw him anyway, would he remember me, I don't want to give him that chance, should I even be thinking of doing this.

BACK TO HOTEL

If I go back to our villa now, that's it for having a day to myself. I did have a great day, went shopping, had a ladies lunch, and walked as much as I could in my Chanel sneakers. I could finesse some more time if I needed it. But what a surprise, because even though I never really want to, I miss him sometimes, especially when I think about how things used to be when we were romantic all the time, day and night, afternoon and evening, dusk and dawn, rain or shine. We've been very romantic lately.

I opened the door. He was watching a car race. Why do they sit there and watch these things. The race has three hundred laps around an oval circle and what, you watch cars go around the same exact circle three hundred times while it makes a horrible buzzing noise? Not knocking the sport – don't get me wrong I think the drivers like Jimmie Johnson and Kyle Busch, Longano, Earnhardt, Montoya oh they are all really impressive - but the bzzzzz bzzzzzzz bzzzzzzzz for four hours is more than I can take for thirty seconds.

"Hi honey," I said, as I walked brusquely into the room because I still had momentum from my walk home.

"Hello my beautiful Cara," Rega said, looking

up to inspect me from head to toe with a smile on his face. "What do you want to do tonight my lovely one?"

Oh he said them, his most endearing words to me, I'm his 'lovely one.' Always makes me feel like I'm a flower, a gorgeous blooming flower. I fall for his flattery too easily.

Before I could answer he motioned for me to sit by his side on the white couch with pale green pillows that perfectly matched the sea foam green walls and eighteen inch diagonally laid stone floor tiles the color of lettuce.

He's reeling me in for something, I feel it. I usually have a good sense for this, but I have no idea where it's going this time.

"Cara, is there someplace in particular you want to go for dinner tonight. I'm thinking we're in Florida, we have to have stone crabs or lobster or red snapper or you know, seafood, let's go out and have seafood. We're at the ocean, in the tropics, we have to have fish, don't you think? We'll find a romantic place by the water. What do you say, my Cara baby."

What do I say? I'd rather just take a walk. "As long as we can take a walk by the ocean in the moonlight when we get back, just you and me, I'm open to anything you feel like doing." If he has the upper hand, which is the only hand he ever likes to have, then maybe I'll be able to figure out what he is up to.

There were flowers and birds pictured on the accessorized décor throughout the villa. The Egyptian cotton sheets were adorned with pale pink roses, blue and red birds. There was a miniature palm tree in the corner. I loved it here.

BUMPING INTO HER

I don't remember ever feeling this awful, yes I do.

I don't know what they are going to do without me, but I have a two week vacation, and even though I take more time off than I should, it is hard to be in France. I can *parler* some *francais* but not enough, they talk too fast, I need slow, *lentement s'il vous plait*, then maybe I can understand and say something meaningful in return.

But where would I go, where would it be right, where can I be myself, feel the best, start all over again, be incognito but out there, under the radar but hyperactive, swinging still, moving leisurely to the sunny darkness, where I can be my nimble nervy self unfettered by the fetter.

When I was a little girl we took family vacations in Miami, but it isn't my ami anymore it's someone else's ami nothing looks the same except the pink sidewalks.

So much to think about. I am so mesmerized by the Mediterranean Sea, I try to memorize all the countries that it touches I am so smart but I can't ever remember them all there are so many it must be a topographical singular phenomenon.

One day I looked it up in the library, how

many countries touch this sea, printed it out in a size ten font, folded the paper into a little rectangle size and put it in my wallet. The paper says that The Mediterranean Sea is connected to the Atlantic Ocean by the Strait of Gibraltar, and touches Albania, Algeria, Bosnia-Herzegovina, Croatia, Cyprus, Egypt, France, Greece, Israel, Italy, Lebanon, Libya, Malta, Morocco, Monaco, Montenegro, Northern Cyprus, Palestine, Slovenia, Spain, Syria, Turkey, and Tunisia – and the British Overseas Territories Gibraltar and Akrotiri and Dhekelia. Who would even know these words, is there anyplace else on the earth where this is possible?

Re everything else, I'll decide later.

Maybe I'll go to Florida, to Delray Beach, Boca Raton, Palm Beach, not one bad choice, I need the warmth and humidity, the little geckos running around like twirlies in a light show.

Or I'll stay in my apartment in New York City where it is like being in one gigantic mall but you live in it in constant motion because it all moves to a beat.

Nobody knows me anywhere I am, I can do what I want, as long as I'm cute, but not too cute.

Why would I want to trade the evocative Mediterranean Sea for the colossal Atlantic Ocean and the narrow Intracoastal edged by mansions and used like a street by boats and yachts who have the right of way so you have to stop whenever the bridges open.

But okay, and *c'est la vie*, now is now, I should not have done what I did but I couldn't help it. It happened last night, when I was leaving the restaurant where I ate alone. I had a few sips of red wine and pretended I was in France on the Côte d'Azur.

I remembered last time I was there, just a few months ago. I walked on the Croisette past the beautiful hotels, the elegant shops, the old convention center, you turn your head one way and see the sea and the beach and restaurants touching the shore line. It's a long walk, but I'm always so comfortable in my black pants, black long sleeve tee shirt, black sneakers and my hair in a ponytail.

Ah the smell, it's the bouquet of the sea, the whiffs hovering because we are surrounded by small mountains,

I walked through the Carlton lobby, then outside to the sidewalk, turned left, turned left again on to the Rue de Canada and ahhh you're away from the middle of it all.

I walked north on the Rue de Canada, towards the maritime alps passing small shops, the Mercure Cannes Croisette Beach Hotel, homes and apartments. A few more blocks and turn left onto the Rue d'Antibes, my catnip, a shopping street for blocks, I am buzzed as if from ten cups of caffeine.

And then I see her. Where has she been, why haven't I seen her in so long, she looks well, but she looks different.

"Hello," I say. She turns, surprised, maybe shocked if I were to be honest about what happened to her face when she saw me. Was I that unexpected, I suppose so but. It's the but of things that are always the moment of realization.

We kiss quickly with a peck on each cheek, after all we are here in Europe.

I thought I was more prepared so again I spoke first. "I'm so happy and surprised to see you," I said.

I didn't want to say that she looked mortified. I just wanted to see how she reacts without clues or cues. She is one of the only people in the world who knows I could be precarious.

She was the head social worker when I spent two months in the asylum. She always told me that she had so much faith in me, even though I knew she knew that wasn't true.

SAMANTHA AND CORTLAND

Samantha had been relaxing in the lobby of the Carlton in Cannes.

You read the newspapers today and you wonder, what is wrong with these men, she thought. When they were little boys they probably all had toy guns, toy army people, toy army tanks and so now they control all of the grown up sized gadgets that crash and make loud noises and cause great harm to people and places. Is it their testosterone that forces them to take that course and play so rough with their big boy gadgets.

They seem to accept this socialized macho power thing as normal. Countries and people need to be armed, war is fine, let's have multi billion dollar companies that exist just to manufacturer the real war toys.

My father wouldn't be in the position he is in if he didn't understand the world in total depth, it's balances of influence and control. Well of course I grew up thinking about these things.

It is impossible to realize that someone wants to kill my father, it's too real, it's too close. I think that I always knew that something like this could happen.

Which is exactly the turning point that I am

in. I need a plan. Cortland will know what to do, she thought. They were to meet at La Mer Bleu at the beach just feet from the Mediterranean.

She prepared to leave the center of her universe, The Carlton in Cannes. As they had planned, they soon met at the top of the seaside walk and stepped down towards the sea on the warn wooden stair slats, and into the restaurant. They were seated with spectacular views of the beach and sea.

He was so cordial. She had no time to waste.

"Cortland, I need your confidence, your expertise and your help," she began.

"Of course, let's talk. We both care for your father more than practically anyone else in the world."

Samantha moved slowly from side to side, comfortable on the chintz rose fabric cushion on a bamboo chair with her navy silk loose long pants with a white and gold stripe going down the sides, with matching Nehru collared jacket. It was one of her own designs, it came in white too. She was always diversifying, spinning.

There were bodies being found here too. Cortland was here because of that, she was sure. She and her father would go home tomorrow. She was ready to go home.

A DAY BRAVER

I'm a day braver than I was yesterday.

My desk is the deepest brown mahogany with two brass swans sitting on it in the right upper corner. I love brass, I collect brass.

I want to go to the other room and talk to him, but I'm afraid of who I am going to be tonight. I'm tired, I'm over tired. I took a two hour nap this afternoon after going to four different appointments.

I hear him moving around in there with the television on one of the all day and night news channels.

RAN I AM

I ran because it was the only thing that I could do. It was the only way to feel it because before this there was only bumping into soft covered walls while trying to figure out what does it mean to be a person.

Am I the I who I think I am, or am I who you think I am.

Should I do what I was doing before or should I do what I'm doing now. There are always choices, I usually make the wrong one.

I can be alone with these thoughts, for minutes, for hours, and then something happens again.

The point is the doorbell rang so I answered it dressed in this really awesome turquoise silk blouse and flowy pants, a white heeled shoe with turquoise stones, and a beautiful necklace with five small diamonds.

I let him come over because let's face it, don't we all like music and art.

But we couldn't stay here. I wanted to go to his house to see his record collection. But I would have to change first, I explained to him. It was raining out now and I didn't want to ruin the silk. He thought I was adorable in my ponytail.

NOT LIKE ANY OTHER DAY

Today started not like every other day. I couldn't stop moving, I can't stop pacing.

I'm pacing because I have too much energy I can't sit. I did three laundries. I'm listening to music, paid a few bills, took a two mile walk, had lunch, went to the pool and did ten laps, took a shower, took a nap.

I really did all that in my mind, because what I was really doing was thinking and planning while I have the news on in the background. I can get so involved in what they're talking about that I just never do anything but this day was going to be different.

I could take a walk. That always leads you to somewhere. I'm wound up. I would like it to stop once and awhile.

When I'm in Florida I'm so slowed down by the heat I'm practically comatose. I'm used to running around all day, that has a name I am sure but I can't do only one thing at a time.

I need the warmth of Florida, the familiarity, the smell, the palm trees, the geckos, the mangrove trees, bougainvillea, jacaranda, royal poinciana, hibiscus, jasmine, everything tropical but of course not the snakes. You can walk down a street and say

222

oh there's a banana tree.

You can cross the street and be on the sand that touches the ocean. It is all so poetic, really, the way everything is connected to everything.

I wondered what would become of me so I wandered through the streets until there was the beach. You can't live without the beach it is what life is.

He grabbed me and told me he loved me. If that were true maybe all of this other stuff would not have happened. I didn't love him either but that was besides the point.

PIPES BURST

I walked to the refrigerator to get the raisins for my oatmeal and when I got there my feet got wet. The electricity must have gone off in the freezer over night and everything defrosted, I thought, so immediately I opened the door but everything inside looked normal.

I looked up. The water was dripping from the ceiling just above where I was standing. I put the pool towel from yesterday right there on the stone floor with a few large pots carefully positioned to catch the drips. I heard more dripping overhead on the right, and then I saw that the entire length of the upper wall of the eat-in kitchen had water stains swaggering across the ceiling.

The plumber dropped the ladder to the attic and went up there looking for the sources of the leak. The pipes were all polybutylene from thirty years ago, which had since been banned, what did they expect, they were going to last forever? There was water in the ceiling and in the walls.

Well that ruined my plans for the day. Oh no, this isn't fair, I'm in the mood, I'm moody today I want to go out and do something. But now I have to deal with this. Like a grown-up, like an organized person.

They cut open the dry wall to get to the pipes to fix them with a metal brace. I called the insurance company and they sent over the men who brought the machines to take the moisture out of the walls and the ceiling because I do not want mildew or mold. The machines are so loud like there's a jet plane in the room.

See what happens when your plans change and you have no idea what your plans are any more but then all of a sudden your new plan appears right before your eyes and it's perfect, you could not have arranged anything better.

If it hadn't been for the pipe burst, I wouldn't have put off going out to do my chores. And if I hadn't put off doing my chores, I would not have met him.

After the contractors left I went to the supermarket, I needed food, a lot of food, a bottle of wine, plus toilet paper, paper towels, juices. All heavy big bulky things. I'm trying to be mindful of the environment so I'm using paper bags and as soon as I got to the parking lot the bag broke. When just then this gallant young man rushed over to help me, and from then I set about to have an experience that I've never had before.

It was a beautiful day. He helped me put everything in the trunk. I said to him, "thank you, thank you so much for your help." He modestly, with his red hair and his green shirt and jeans said, "oh really, it was no big deal."

"But it was a big deal to me," I explained to him. "I have an idea. I'm starving, most of this food can be for a picnic. Why don't we go to Island Beach, I'll open my blanket and we'll celebrate how you helped me."

Well, he thought I was the cutest most charming, and obviously irresistible girl, so he said, "yes, sure, why not. That's a really great idea. I really appreciate it, I'm hungry too."

I'm so clever, he didn't know that no one went to Island Beach at this hour, and anyway I would find someplace secluded behind the dunes and the boulders, way off the walking path. By the time he realized what I had in mind, after eating three sandwiches and washing it down with wine, the breeze was filling the carved flowers on his chest with so much sand that it actually started to look three dimensional.

What a talent I am. I didn't know I could be this impressed with myself.

DEBRIS RAINED DOWN

The debris rained down, furiously and unexpectedly. What were those trillions of particles so blue and iridescent that it was at once beautiful and frightening because what was it.

It wasn't snow, it wasn't hail, it wasn't rain. It was shiny blue, seductive to behold, made of something softer and smaller than jelly bellies. They pile up on the ground.

Everyone stopped what they were doing and tried to figure out what was happening. Was this over the rainbow or the road to some kind of netherworld. What were they saying about it on the radio and television.

What an imagination I have. I created an entire scenario because a delivery truck's cargo of candy just spilled on the streets and sidewalks.

Well, that certainly took my mind off of what was really happening here, right now. The blood is all over the place.

FRIENDS ARE GONE

All of my friends are dying I hardly know who I am anymore. They define me, they love me, they got a kick out of me. That's how I knew I was great. No no, don't misunderstand me, I didn't do it, no, never, not to my friends. They just went by themselves.

Now I have to figure out what to do with the rest of my life.

I keep making the same mistakes. Over and over again. I'm like gum under my own shoes. I really try but nothing I do works. I just can't stop it.

Maybe I'll call that cute guy I used to go out with. He still thinks I'm really something, loved the blouse I wore last time I saw him at that dinner party I was acting so normal he of all people could never imagine. Decades ago we had a good relationship, we were both cheating on someone else, it was mean, it was nervy, it was really actually not so good. But he was cute and very smart, and I was cute and very smart, it is hard to resist cute and smart.

I don't like it when I have too many decisions to make, I don't like being overwhelmed, but then again, I can figure out how to handle this, I always figure things out.

WALK AROUND THE CIRCLE

I don't know how many times I've walked around this circle but I've been walking around this circle for a while now.

We are all just babies, don't you get it. Our bodies get bigger and grow older, but maybe we don't.

SLOW RAIN

It was just one of those slow rains, the kind that makes you feel like it is humming in your ear you want to be cuddled by it. I wanted to take my clothes off and hide under the blankets for about forever.

This would be a good way to avoid the day, this would be one of the reasons we left home to go on vacation, this could let me not see his friends. But that's not going to happen.

There was a quiet knock on my door, I said who is it, he said it's me. He wanted to know if I thought he should get a hair cut. Of the thousand things that were on my mind at that moment, that wasn't even on the list.

CARA WALLS

I keep clothes for ten years, even more, so that I can pretend that time has not moved too far or so fast.

There are so many little lizards today, those straight tailed racers and the ones with the curly tails. The curly tailed guys just don't care, they have attitude, they'll just stand there and stare you down holding their position on the path that you are trying to walk on to the pool, they scare me, I think they could pounce and sting. The other ones, they just scamper fast at the sight and sound of you.

I've seen snakes a few times, at least two are living on the right side of the path as you leave our villa.

He gives me a good life, but I'm restless. If I sit in the sun for a while and then swim a few laps maybe the stress will calm. I can't sit still, it's worse than it's ever been.

And of course I have a new outfit. I'll put it on, he will melt, we'll have a wonderful wine with escargots. That's the kind of magic moments we can have together. Otherwise we are a strange pairing, he made the moves to make sure it happened, and it worked.

The birds are beautiful here. The white haired

long beaked ibis's come out by the dozens after a rain digging their noses in the ground looking for worms. I see long necked blue herons walking along the lake on the grounds, they are elegant.

Tonight his friends are stopping by and it's not like we're home on Long Island in our gated mansion where I can be five rooms away. Here I'm right behind a wall and a door.

The ducks look like they're looking for their friends. The large turtles cross the street and you have to get out of your car and carry the slow walkers to the sidewalk. They're looking for water. Sometimes there's a woodpecker and big bright green foot long lizards, they're like little dragons, they're so nonchalant.

I try to make things seem like everything's okay, I do. Rega never thinks that anything is on my mind, I can be so blasé.

But I am telling you that if anything is going to change my life, affect my life in any way at all, I want to know about it right now, and he's not telling me but there is something happening. I like my big house, all my clothes, we travel, we eat out, we have a car and driver when we want that, what, what else do I want I don't want anything to change.

I'll try to wait till after dinner to say anything, he needs to be relaxed so it doesn't seem like I'm prying.

I'm walking on the path. What's Paul doing here, why did Rega bring him to Florida. He was supposed to be in the house taking care of things. He's usually so shy, why is he here.

"Hello, Mrs. Rega," he said in his reluctant mannerly way.

"Well, hello Paul. What a surprise to see you here." I paused and then needed to know, and thought I would try to take advantage of his meekness, "what in the world brings you here?"

"Oh, Mrs. Rega, just some work for Mr. Rega."

"But why here, I thought you had responsibilities in the house."

"Well yes ma'am, of course, yes of course I do. I can't really answer because I haven't sat with Mr. Rega to talk about details."

He was watching my face.

"Well then, you better go and meet with him," and with that he kept walking.

I didn't want to miss this, so I followed him.

I walked in to the villa, said hello and excused myself explaining that I had to change for dinner. I walked into my closet and admired myself in the wrap around mirrors.

I had everything ready in case I had this chance, these small microphones that could hear through the wall recording onto a special CD. Just as insurance for myself. What else could I do.

SO I BOPPED

So I bopped on the hillside all the day long, telling him how much I loved him while I'm singing this song.

I brought my portable radio, he brought the wine. We put a bedspread on the living room floor of his apartment and pretended we were outside.

We could have so much more fun inside.

TAN LINES

I don't think I have a temper. I don't yell. I calm down and it's over. Really, I tend to under-exaggerate.

I get upset if I use too much water, there are people who are thirsty. I get upset if I vote and maybe my vote didn't count because I bothered to read about who is running. I'm late sending birthday cards, but there is no timetable on belated.

I can be my inert with inertia self at the pool, I don't have iguana arms yet, so I put on my bikini bathing suit because there is nothing like tan lines. And I have to always have something that is tantalizing.

I HAVE TO TELL YOU THIS

Look, I have to tell you this. I am not who you think I am. Almost, but not quite. Really, you have to listen to me or you won't see what's happening, like if you miss an episode of a television series – you just can't miss anything.

AS WAS MY CUSTOM

As was my custom every night before drawing my bath, I review the evening because in my reverie I can be anywhere and anyone. I was sitting now on the veranda of our villa, the Atlantic Ocean shimmering neath the moon with boat lights near and far to the horizon. It was the season, everyone was here.

He loves no other but me, that I always know. My man, what would he do without me, I can't imagine.

The rest of the gist to know is that it's all about your attitude and bothering to figure things out, it's your choice to react one way or another.

Because what happened then was surely something that not a soul who ever walked this mud could ever have conjured.

I just know that you know in that place just beneath your chest what is truth.

If I had bumped into Samantha in Cannes, we surely would have had tea in the lobby of the Carlton. And she would have told me too much without meaning to because I was so sure I was that alluring.

I found it interesting, that I was right there in front of them but not.

She was here just to get away for a few days, under her father's watch. She needed to breathe, to run around a little after being so locked in. Where are her watchers flanking her, I didn't see anything that looked like that.

REGA SAID TOO MUCH

Cortland rarely did much on his hours off except visit Amy. But this week he was invited to a birthday dinner for his Uncle Joe at one of his favorite seafood restaurants on Long Island, the Jolly Fishtown. He was overjoyed, he hadn't had lobster in a while, and they had the best.

Friends and family of Joe had a table for ten near the window that overlooked the scenic duck pond. It was a clear spring evening, it was still light out. No matter where your table was located on the enclosed patio, you could see the beauty out there. But only the tables near the windows could see the entire park.

The advantage to having such a great table was the view. The disadvantage was that throughout the meal, patrons from other tables would walk over to stand next to your table to get a better view. The park had five different ponds, each surrounded by lawns, and with a small island within each pond reachable by a narrow wooden walking bridge. It was such a lovely evening, there were people strolling with their baby carriages and dogs on leashes, and there were ducks paddling in the waters.

While Uncle Joe was making small talk with his guests, two men walked from their table across the room to the window, talking non-stop in tones they obviously intended to be hushed, but both of their voices carried enough that Cortland, whose seat was right at that window, could hear every word.

One of the men was wearing a navy blue blazer with gold buttons, a white shirt, jeans and white sneakers. The other wore a black sports jacket with a black silk shirt, black pants and black shoes. Cortland was trained to be observant.

"That mother fucker takes all the credit all the time. He never tried to find me to thank me, in all these years, do you believe that, after what I did for him. The ungrateful prick. If I hadn't been protecting him, he would never have gotten this far, he would have had no peace. I gave him that."

"Okay, okay," said the navy blazer, "so why didn't you stay in touch with him, sounds like it's your fault, why are you complaining now."

"Because we moved away, I was young, I didn't know how to get in touch with him, and he never got in touch with me, so we lost touch, and later I didn't know where to find him, and later than that I was blocked from finding him. Our goddamn government, protecting their own. He never would have become such a big shot if it wasn't for me, you're damn right I threatened him. He needs to make it right with me."

"We shouldn't talk about this here, Rega, we just shouldn't."

"Why, you think there are spooks here knowing that we were going to be in this restaurant on this night, just waiting to hear what we have to say?" said the man in black.

Well, turns out there was. Cortland heard every word and while he figured this could just be one of those bizarre coincidences, really you never know. He was thinking that there really could not possibly be such a thing as a needle in a haystack, except when there is. And for an agent of his caliber, this was too interesting to let go.

As the two men returned to their table, Cortland discretely took pictures of them with his small pocket camera, and later used his government badge to ask the restaurant's owner for their names.

WRITING TO BILLY

If I hadn't been writing to Billy, I might have had too much time on my hands to do other things that I probably should not do my needs are too severe. Billy Blue Light I call him, because there's a blue dot next to each new email, and he has been writing a lot lately because he thinks I'll want to meet him. But I don't, I just need someone to talk to.

I'm so used to writing to him every day, I tell him everything and I tell him nothing. It's a connection, the only just cerebral one that I have. I'll never meet him, that's better for him of course.

Billy was sweeter than the honeydew, his messages were like soft breezes that collect molten gusts on their way to you he was trying too hard. What do you do with that.

After spilling no beans with him, I had to get things off my chest. So I turned the computer off, put on my black pants, black long sleeve tee shirt, black thin cotton socks, and black rubber soled suede shoes with no laces.

I ran down the street with abandon, opened my voice, deep and resonant, and sang my favorite songs, then I conversed with myself in French because if you just read it and you don't hear it and speak it, you'll lose it. *C'est bon.*

It's getting late, I forgot to eat lunch, I'm starving. I decided to go to the Night Bird.   They have a piano bar there, I love piano bar music.

I ordered a burger medium well with gruyere cheese and caramelized onion what could be better. I finished it with a vanilla egg cream, I wasn't in the mood to get sleepy from wine I was feeling peppy.

I love those songs, "Strangers In The Night," "Go Away Little Girl," everything that could remind me of me. I'm here with just a few couples and a few men. I've been bored, my employers are away for two more days so I have hours and hours for myself.

I was tapping my fingers to "Chattanooga Choo Choo" when my eye was caught by someone watching me who was tapping his fingers to the same beat. Oh yes, nothing like being in sync.

I'm in no hurry, I am so in no hurry I have time to relax and I am relaxed. Some people are in a hurry, and evidently this man was he didn't want to wait to meet me he wanted to meet me now.

He walked over as "I'll Never Smile Again" was playing and I thought, well, this could be prophetic for him. But you never know, let's see how it goes.

"Hi, are you expecting someone, can I sit here with you?" he asked.

"I don't know you, so how am I to know if I want your company."

"Let's give it a try. I'm here alone, you're here alone. Maybe we could just enjoy the music together."

I looked him over, he was nice looking, he looked like he had accomplished some things in his life. Might as well find out what.

Turns out he works for the library, he loves books. I told him I was in pharmaceuticals. After that we just talked about the music.

He was drinking wine, I was drinking apple juice in a wine glass with no ice, no lemon, no lime so it looked like white wine, let him think we are both on the same wave length.

I told him that I came here twice a month, I love hearing the old songs on the piano. He was delighted to tell me that he lived just two blocks away. Would I like to come over for a nightcap and to see his record collection, he's got all the old songs.

I told him I found that suggestion irresistible. He liked that response. He had an old fashioned record player and a great collection of LPs with the songs from the 40's and 50's.

We listened to a few albums, we danced and giggled. And then, when he was too drowsy from the wine, he lay his back on the couch hoping I would join him saying let's rest for awhile and then we'll dance more later. I did join him on the couch, much to his eternal surprise. When he realized that he would probably never dance again, I could see the gloomy look on his face, I could tell he thought he was such a good judge of character, he was so surprised.

But the designs on him were really my best, I think that practice does make perfect, they were getting more complex. I should be taking my own pictures for a coffee table book, who's my competition. So I did, I took a picture of his outstanding floral chest.

Just then "You Always Hurt The One You Love" played as I said to him isn't that so true. He had told me his name was Carl. I said I love you Carl, I really do, I'm so sorry we didn't dance again but I just can't help it because my name is Rita.

CORTLAND CALLS BRENNER

As soon as Cortland got into his car after dinner, he called Brenner.

"You know how sometimes we get leads and sometimes we don't and sometimes when we do they come from strange unexpected places," Cortland crowed.

"Yes, that's how it happens most of the time, or so it seems," replied Brenner.

"You're so right my friend, you're so right," said Cortland.

"So what's going on here, what are you so happy about, it better be good I was just having a nap," Brenner responded.

"It might be good and it might be nothing. But even if it's not for our case I have a feeling that it's going to be good for something."

"Let's have it already." Brenner implored jovially.

"Let me just say in advance that I want to solve this so badly, maybe I am just reading into this because I need to. I need to get this resolved for Heywood, for GRETA, for Samantha, for my Amy, for our nation."

"I know how much this means to you Cortland, to all of us. What did you hear?" Brenner asked again.

"There was this man, in the restaurant where I was having dinner tonight. He was talking a lot louder than he should have been, he has one of those voices that just carries, and I happened to be sitting right there."

"You're dragging this out, Cortland. Please, get to the point. Now you got me so curious."

"Look, I know we can't imagine the whole story about this one yet, but I heard something and I just got a feeling. And I have pictures."

Cortland told him everything that he heard, and immediately sent the details and pictures into Brenner and GRETA.

THE BOYFRIEND

Cortland brought the folder containing the information Douglas Heywood had requested about Samantha's boyfriend. Heywood should not have been concerned, Colter thought, although a father understandably reacts far differently about personal issues than does a government mogul about official business.

Heywood was pleased to find that Andre Jardin's family was, in fact, one of the more accomplished and well-to-do families in France. Seems the father was a French government attaché, a specialist in both cultural and military concerns, assigned to various missions over the years, plus he was involved with importing and exporting select high end products. Kindred, perhaps we speak the same language, Heywood thought.

"But what does the son do?" he asked Cortland. "His pedigree sounds good, but what did he do with it."

"Well, seems like he took quite a different route, but with some notoriety. But with some leanings also in his father's direction."

"That was a circumventing response, Cortland. Please, just come out with it," replied Heywood.

"He showed noteworthy musical talents at an early age," offered Cortland. "His parents couldn't deny it. And although they evidently had imagined him following in his father's footsteps, his aptitude for music was obvious. So of course, as most parents would, they encouraged him."

"Did he make a career of that?" questioned Heywood.

"He became an important music publisher. In fact he heads one of the most important music publishing operations in all of Europe."

"Well, that sounds impressive," Heywood thought out loud.

"It is. And although we hear that he is quite the virtuoso on keyboards, he decided to stay on the business side of the music business."

"I must admit that I am always impressed with people who have both a business and creative penchant. I've always wanted to play an instrument, I tried when I was young, but I was never good at it."

After some moments of thought, Heywood continued, "I can understand more now how Samantha could find this appealing, and surely he would find her beguiling just for herself, and also as her family shares similar interests as his own."

The two men changed the subject for awhile, talking about world issues that always fascinated and disturbed them, but about which they always treasured the other's perspective.

Then Heywood continued. "Now that I can rest a bit easier about this Andre Jardin, I have to admit that I am still not sure why she waited so long to tell me about him."

"Probably because she knows you are going through so much right now, and she merely wanted to be sure before she made such an important announcement."

"I suppose you're right, Cortland." Heywood hesitated before he continued. "I guess I'm just not used to her having someone in her life. I've waited for this moment for her, for her happiness, I just want to feel certain that he is indeed the very best for her."

Now that they had the personal discussion handled, at least for now, Cortland was ready to tell Heywood about the possible connection between what he heard in the restaurant and the threat that Heywood had received. He thought also that today would be the right time to tell Heywood that he was going to ask Amy to marry him. But he decided to wait until after they had their lunch, so they would both be sufficiently fortified to delve into it all.

YOU WALKED

I worshipped the ground you walked on. I put you on the highest pedestal. I defended you against the awful truth time and again because I needed to, I wanted you to be my dream but you never really were. You hurt me with a ferocity that you should never do to a human girl. I don't know why I thought that was love.

You left us on the side of the road with no ride. I kept hailing a cab that never stopped for me, I thought maybe they just didn't see me I must be invisible.

How much can one person take, someone keeps testing the edges to see how much she can take. Well guess what, finally she just can't take anymore. That's when the bridges burned, the gates crashed, the dams imploded, the barricades tumbled.

You can't dress that up, it will ooze through the pores of it, cascade onto the shores of it, rain on the parade of it.

You promised you would always watch over me but you didn't. So I'm here and I know it but you don't.

You beat the shit of it, it couldn't hardly breath anymore. Trickle trickle went the tears, you just walked away, you didn't even turn around to see what happened, I was left to do it all.

What do you think, I really am normal I just act like this sometimes but not all the time, isn't that redeeming? Who else would be normal and act like this. Come on now, I don't ever want to be just one in the crowd, I need to stand out.

What if they catch me one day, so what if they do. What would they do to me, give me an award for originality, I guess. I can tell by what they write about me in the papers that there just has never been anyone else like me.

I don't have too much time left, I know it, so I need to make the best of what's left of it all.

What are you doing tonight, we could get together.

BECOMING LOCAL

The phone rang in Colter's office. It was Interpol, they had something they wanted to share.

"Okay we're on it," Colter said to the Interpol agent. "I'll get back to you as soon as we get something."

"We finally have information to go on," he told Grange as he ran into his office.

Grange's office was messy as ever while his fingers rat-tat-tatted on his desk. His thick brown hair and bushy eyebrows were just sitting there waiting to be combed.

"What's going on," Grange asked. His partner Colter from Special Investigations didn't run down the hall for no reason.

"Seems that two men had dinner in a restaurant on Long Island. A conversation was overheard by a Fed, who just happened to be eating there too. He thought something sounded suspicious about it, worth looking into."

Well, that explains it, they both thought, when there's a local element, we're who they call.

"We have one name, and we have a picture," Colter continued. He showed Grange the picture of the two men in the restaurant, and identified one of them.

"The one in the navy blazer is Elliot Turnby, he lives on Long Island and Palm Beach."

"So what's the story, why is this interesting."

"Seems that the Feds are looking for someone who has been threatening someone high up in government. They're not telling us who is being threatened at this time. This Fed happened to be in easy earshot of the conversation, thought he heard something fishy. But we know, when you're on a case, everything can sound fishy. But they want us to look into this person, see who his friends are, see if we can identify the man he was talking to, because the one who he's talking to is the one who said the suspicious things."

Colter told Grange everything that was explained to him. About the restaurant, the view, where the Fed was sitting, what he heard, why it might relate to an investigation the Feds are doing.

"Yeah, I've been to that restaurant, they do have great seafood," Grange recalled, while he was clearly digesting all that Colter was saying.

Colter was wearing his trademark tan pants, plaid shirt, blazer and loafers, his inexpensive off-the-rack version of Ivy League, but he wore it well.

"Okay, let's run this," Colter said.

About an hour later they had reams of read-outs on Elliot Turnby: addresses, businesses, clubs, pictures. But nothing that could lead to the second man.

"Okay," Colter said. "It's a start. At least we know some of what we're looking for here."

"Yeah," said Grange, "this is a good start." He looked at the picture they received from Interpol. "This one in the all black, he looks like a character from a movie. Too bad this Fed wasn't able to get a napkin or a glass that he used. Too bad. We could have had some science."

REGA TELLS ELLIOT WHY

"Not even Cara knows about any of this," Rega said. "Not even my Cara."

"No? How is that possible?" asked Rega's friend Elliot Turnby. "I can't believe you never told her."

"Sure you can believe it. What business was it of anyone's, huh? What business. That was another lifetime ago."

"When exactly did you do it?"

"You know, after my parents died, my aunt and uncle took me to finish raising me. I was only about thirteen, really young. Too young, I missed my parents so much, but my aunt and uncle didn't give a shit."

Rega and Elliot Turnby were sitting in Rega's den in his house on Long Island.

"Is this what's going on with you lately, Rega?" Elliot asked. "Ever since we had dinner at the Jolly Fishtown you've been like a crazy angry kid."

"I am angry, and I have a million reasons to be."

They decided to take a ride to the Hampshire Inn and have a drink in the lounge there, where they were seated at a private table in the back. They wanted to be able to get into this more without the possibility of anyone walking in to interrupt them.

After ordering their drinks, they continued their conversation.

"Okay, so you're trying to tell me that you changed your name and you threatened someone in the government?" Elliot asked.

"Yeah, that's what I'm trying to tell you." Rega responded.

"You have totally lost me, my friend. Well, tell me about it, tell me all about it." Elliot was thinking that his friend wasn't just the quirky person he thought he was. He was beginning to realize that he was about to hear something pretty wacky. He took a breath and asked, "Which one are you going to tell me first?"

"The name thing. I'll tell you the name thing first," Rega said. They both had a few sips of their drinks before Rega began.

Rega cleared his throat, and then started to explain. "Okay, so I was young when my parents died in that car accident, only about thirteen. My mother's sister, my Aunt May and her husband closed the apartment, threw out most of my parent's belongings, and took me away to live with them. It was like moving to another planet."

"What do you mean," asked Elliot.

"Well, in the old neighborhood we had sidewalks, we had street lights. Here, on Long Island, I didn't know where to walk, there were no sidewalks. And where I used to live you knew you were supposed to come home for dinner when the street lights went on. There were no street lights."

"Sounds nice, what was the problem."

"Those really weren't problems. The problem was they didn't give a shit about me. I moved away from all my friends and my neighborhood, and I didn't know how to reach anyone, and they didn't care. There were no emails yet. It was like they just wanted me to forget that I had a past, forget my old friends, and just be the star in their lives, as if that is when my life started, the selfish bastards," he said with palpable anger.

"Did they have kids of their own?"

"No, I was it for them. So they put it all on me, I was supposed to make them happy, to hell with what I wanted."

"So did they give you a good life?" Elliot asked.

"No, they gave me a terrible life, it was all about them."

They had ordered baked mozzarella sticks with their drinks, and stopped a minute to eat some.

Rega continued, "So yes, I was so mad all the time that I started to get into some trouble. Trouble in school, trouble with the law, I was a juvenile and I had a record already. One thing after another, I was a maniac. But then when I reached a certain age, thank god I said to myself this is no good, you have to make something of yourself. So I left them, I left them and never looked back and never got in touch with them again. I wanted to start fresh, so I changed my name."

"You mean Robert Rega isn't your real name?" Elliot asked with calm astonishment.

"No, no it's not, but it's a good name, isn't it. I always liked it. I think it fits me. I figured if I ever met someone who I wanted to marry, or go into business with, I just didn't want to have a bad rap behind me. Know what I mean?"

"Well okay, I can get that. I can." Elliot said. No one spoke for a few minutes. They just sipped on their drinks and ate a bit. Then Elliot asked him, "So what was your name before, what's your real name, Rega. I still can't believe it's not Robert Rega."

"My name was Tony. Tony Camera." They didn't speak for a few more minutes, letting this new information sink in.

"So then I wanted to start a new life. I tried to think of a business to get into that was a necessity, that everybody wanted and everybody needed. So I started importing products. Liquor was the first one, I figured everybody drinks, it could only be good, it will last for years, take care of my whole life. But that wasn't enough so I kept adding other things, not everything so legal it turns out, but I needed to keep making money." He always knew he had to pull off some down and dirty things to make it all work, he didn't become a boy scout. Always a closet maniac.

"But you did good with it all, real good," Elliot commented, knowing that that's exactly how the two of them met. "Look, there are a lot of us shady guys working all the time. We look great on the outside, but we're just hustling all the time to keep something going. We're living good, so we're doing good."

"Yeah, that's it. You gotta be a street fighter." Then Rega paused, and thought out loud, "But you see, for me, I can't brush it, I know I should have done better. I had it right there, I was sort of involved with things that became real respectable. I could have been a government advisor, really up and up, and they ruined that for me," Rega opined.

Elliot looked at him incredulously. "Where in the hell did that come from?" he asked.

"Well, that's the other part of this whole thing. That's the other part. That's where maybe I put myself in big trouble. Very big trouble. It's been a lot of years since I've been in big trouble. But sometimes, you know, sometimes I get a mean temper and do something crazy. And I did that."

The two men sat there for a minute. Then Elliot asked, "Okay, what did you do?"

Rega realized that Elliot would probably have no idea how to take what he was about to tell him. But he needed to be able to talk to somebody about this, cause he certainly couldn't talk to any of his own men about anything. And he would never tell Cara about any of this.

"You're really the first person that I've ever told all of this to," Rega said.

Elliot braced himself for he didn't know what.

And then Rega continued, "I think how you take it depends on where you grew up. Where did you grow up, Elliot?"

"Why, why does it matter?"

"I understand if this sounds crazy to you, but it matters because if you didn't know street life, if you didn't know the streets, if you never had to deal with the street mentality, you won't understand."

"You got hurt by the streets?"

"Yeah, I found out early that I had to hold my own all the time. Otherwise I would get insulted, beaten up. Otherwise I would get taken advantage of. That's why I'm such an angry bastard all the time. I got pushed around too much when I was younger. I had to learn how to be tough."

"What set you off on this now?"

"Well I started feeling slighted again, real slighted, and I didn't like it."

"Yeah, so?"

"Yeah, so, I got really pissed at someone and I did something really stupid about it."

"What, you killed someone?"

"No, I didn't kill anyone. But I got so out of control that I threatened someone's life."

"Who, whose life."

"Someone important in the government."

"Why? Why would you do something so stupid?"

"Cause he became important. There weren't a lot of articles about him, because a lot of what he does is secret government kind of stuff, I got that picture a long time ago. But I helped him get started with it all, he never tried to thank me. I know, I totally know, that if it wasn't for me, he would never have been able to do what he did in the world. I made it possible for him."

"I'll fall for it, what's the deal here?" Elliot asked.

"It all happened because he was smart, but I was tough."

"So how did you learn how to be tough?"

"By protecting him, that's how. And that's what this is all about."

ARE YOU DRESSED

When I stay in my New York City apartment I have so much on my mind, so much to do, I live alone there so I'm always thinking thinking thinking so that I stay organized.

I go out and think did I remember to put my pants on, I'm afraid to look down, I have nobody to check me out I can't remember everything.

Why is everyone looking at me, I look down, oh whew, I am dressed, it could be easy to forget.

I can't forget my keys. I did that once when I was doing my laundry in the basement and I had to go to the building office in my short shorts I was mortified.

You can't walk out without your clothes or your keys.

My life looks more like a kaleidoscope than a newsreel. And now the person I see in the mirror does not look like the person I was.

They say you have to learn from your mistakes, but what if you never make mistakes how are you supposed to learn anything.

I am voguey chic with my enormous black sunglasses and black bag. I am sauntering and sashaying up the avenue needing to fulfill my deprivation but only I know that. A French morsel

would do, something like escargot but larger, much
larger.

REGA CAUGHT

It was a two department two universe achievement. Cortland and Brenner from GRETA, and New York detectives Colter and Grange, tracked Rega down and put together the situation to bring him in. It was easy once they identified Elliot Turnby in the picture.

Elliot Turnby was a dapperly dressed attorney who never had a problem double-crossing anyone, albeit in the most charming ways, if they tried to slow his ability to make money. The only client he had was himself, he was the only person he was interested in protecting. And it worked. While nothing he did was discernibly illegal, he knew where the edge was and how to stay on it for his own advantage.

Rega was the only other person he ever advised about legal matters, not that Rega ever realized that he was actually an attorney. He thought Elliot just knew a lot about these things.

But that's how the Feds got Rega. They had a letter FedExed to his house that seemed to be from a prospective new client that he had been trying to snare. They were importing laptop computers from China, they would sell them to Rega for almost nothing and Rega could vend them for whatever he wanted to charge.

He had to commit to the first order of a couple of thousand machines, and had forty-eight hours to let them know, otherwise they would give it to someone else. After that he could order whatever he wanted whenever he wanted. Rega didn't like to be told how much to order, when to order, he didn't like to be told anything. He knew there could be big money in this tech stuff from China so he wanted to get involved. But he didn't want to get hurt, so he asked Elliot to meet him for lunch so they could talk it over. Maybe Elliot would want to go into it with him.

Colter and Grange arranged for the surveillance on both Rega's and Elliot's homes, and had them followed till they had their lunch. That's how they were able to get Rega on his way home. It was simple, it was peaceful, why couldn't they all be like that.

Rega was driving his Cadillac on the road that lead to his house, but he was still far enough from the house that nobody there would hear or see the commotion. They pulled him over as if for a traffic ticket. The two strongmen jumped out of their car, each grabbed a doorknob on Rega's car, opened it from both sides, and identified themselves as federal officers. Rega immediately knew this was it, what could he do, he couldn't run. They had a third man take his car from the side of the road and bring it in, they put him in the back of their car, and that was that.

He didn't fight them, he didn't argue with them. He just got in the car as he was told, with handcuffs that he hadn't had on since he was a teenager constantly in trouble.

He had done it again, messed up, but even worse than those years ago. This was international, this was government, this was threatening a respected life. He knew what he did.

Why, just to get his attention. The standard looking Dodge with the dark windows didn't let anyone see who was in the back seat. He would save face, at least for this hour.

It was childish, it was felonious, it was wrong. He thought he had his temper under control, but it was always there, it was always ready to burst. He knew it, but he couldn't control it. That was why he changed his name, so he could be somebody new, just a good guy.

He realized too late what could happen to him. If somebody told me they were going to do something like this, I woulda told them they were an idiot. I'm the idiot. I just wanted the thanks and respectability and some money too would be nice. If his parents hadn't died, if his aunt and uncle hadn't taken him, he would have been that person. Now I'll probably be locked up for life, he thought.

He had no idea where they were going, he was in the back seat with the dark windows and a barricade blocking his view out the front. When they ushered him out of the car they were in the basement of a building. They walked him to an elevator, put him in a room with no windows and told him he had to wait to be questioned. There was a bottle of water and a bathroom.

Not too bad, totally unexpected and certainly not quite what he was used to, Rega thought.

CORTLAND CALLS HEYWOOD

Heywood had been relaxing at home when he got the secure call from Cortland.

"We got him. We found the person who threatened you," Cortland told him.

"All because you went out to eat one night?" Heywood said with amazement.

"Yes, it would seem so, my friend," Cortland said with relief.

"If all the other world problems could be solved this easily, what a different world it would be. And there would have been no need for all my ingenuity," Heywood said. Then he continued, "Thank goodness, that little nightmare is over. Who in the world could it be, what in the world was that all about?"

"You're not going to believe this," Cortland answered. "It's a really sad and pathetic story, but I think this will mean something to you. Please understand, I don't want to tell you on the phone. I'd like to come over later."

"What on earth are you talking about, Cortland. You're not making any sense. You caught a criminal and you suspect that I might feel touched by it?" asked Heywood.

"We're going to question him now. I'll call

you and drive to see you after that."

THEY VISIT REGA

They didn't know what kind of thug they were about to meet. All they knew was it seemed that this was the man who had threatened Heywood and his family, and this was the man who caused Amy to be kidnapped and tortured.

Colter and Grange understood that this was Cortland's case, and he would take the lead. They would just listen in case there was local follow-up for them to do.

Rega had just been held for over an hour before they arrived. He had been searched thoroughly, and allowed to keep his street clothes on for the initial interrogations.

"You know that you are here because you threatened a man's life. What do you have to say about that," Cortland began.

"I know I did. I'm a jerk," Rega replied.

"So you admit that you threatened the life of Douglas Heywood?"

"Yes, yes I admit that. Yes, I told you, I'm a jerk."

Well, that was an odd response, Cortland thought.

"Why would you threaten Douglas Heywood?" Cortland asked.

"You don't know? I thought you Feds could find out anything," Rega chided.

"Don't be a wise guy, let's get through this as painlessly as possible," Cortland continued, before I bash in your head for what you did to my Amy, he wanted to say, but didn't. He pretended amity for now in order to be able to get more information.

They were sitting around an old wooden table with uncomfortable wooden chairs. Everyone had a small plastic bottle of water. It was a good prop, a sip was a good stall, and sometimes a needed quench. The only fear was someone throwing their bottle, that's a heavy missile at fast speed and close range.

"Yes, yes, I did that. I sent a stupid threatening note to Douglas Heywood. And I get that you have no idea why I did that."

"Suppose you tell us," Cortland said.

Rega was looking down at his black loafers, as if he were making up something to say, but instead he surprised them because it sounded like he was actually trying to tell them something real.

"Okay, here's the story. Do you want the real story?" Rega asked.

He was uncharacteristically calm and collected for a man who has committed international crimes and who will probably go to prison for the rest of his life, Cortland thought. What is this.

"It's really simple and stupid," Rega began.

"Okay, here goes." Rega wiped his sweating brow.

He told them about his childhood in Flushing, Queens, where his best friend was Douggie, a young Douglas Heywood. They sat rapt at his story, which of course was being taped and monitored.

"I was this strong, tough kid, full of myself. And Douggie was this scrawny thing with a big brain. The other boys always teased him, tried to beat him up and hurt him. I didn't have the brain but I had the tough."

Rega took a sip of his water, then continued. "So I protected him. I walked with him to and from school for five years. From when we were about eight years old till we were about thirteen, I guess."

They all listened intently, with looks on their faces like they were in the wrong room. This was like the area in the library where the teacher told stories to elementary school children, not what they expected.

They could tell he was very nervous, but Rega was being matter of fact trying to get it all out. He had just had a dress rehearsal talking about most of this with his friend Elliot, but this was the real deal. It was clear to him now, and although it probably didn't matter anymore because his life was already ruined, he needed to keep talking.

"Then one day, just like that, my parents were killed. In a car accident."

He wiped his brow again. "My aunt and uncle came to get me, got rid of everything that mattered to me, took me to a new town and wouldn't let me stay in touch with anyone from the neighborhood. Then after that, for years all I did was get in trouble in school and the law."

They felt like they were in a psychiatry session, they had been trained for that too, but they kept feeling like no, this can't be it, something is going to explode here.

"I was a pissed off kid, do you blame me. I was pissed all the time, every slight set me off."

Cortland couldn't take the pablum anymore, so he asked, "What does any of this have to do with now, with the threatening letter you wrote to Heywood?"

"I was a jealous kid, everybody seemed to have it good but me." He took another sip of his water.

"Even though I've had a pretty successful life since then, the thing that made me most proud, in my whole life, was the way I protected my friend Douggie all those years ago. I don't know if you can understand that, I don't know if you are from the streets."

"I still don't get it," said Cortland.

"Even though you all tried to keep his name quiet, I've heard the stories about the great Douglas Heywood, all his inventions, how important he is.

The young genius spends his childhood working on technology that changed the world. Well guess what. If it wasn't for me, he would not have been able to do that."

Rega paused to make sure they were paying enough attention to him, then he continued. "If it wasn't for me, he would have gotten teased and beaten and hurt really bad. But it was me, I'm the one who was there with him, I protected him from all of that, so he could do his important work that he is famous for now. And when they took me away, when my aunt and uncle took me away, all I had left was the trouble I kept getting into. It wasn't fair. It was never fair."

The men found it hard not to look at him like he was out of his mind, and gave each other subtle glances that asked that very thing.

"So why didn't you stay in touch with each other?" Cortland asked.

"That's easy for you to say now, with your internet. We didn't have any of that then, I had no idea how to be in touch with him. We were young."

Then he went on, "When I finally heard about him years later and tried to find him, I was blocked, by the government, it's my government too, they kept him hidden. I even said that we were best childhood friends, but nobody cared. I thought he was dissing me too. I tried everything I could think of. I couldn't find him, I couldn't get to him. I got more and more pissed." He looked around for some understanding, but didn't see any.

"I changed my name because I wanted a new life, a good life," he went on. "I wanted more, I was tired of feeling so bad, but the streets never left me."

"But here's the thing," Rega continued. "I doubt if you understand how important my protecting him was to everything that Heywood landed up accomplishing."

Rega paused for a minute, looked around for some agreement, and then said, "I always felt that if I hadn't picked him up off the ground from the playground that day, and protected him from then on every day for those years, till I had to move, his life would have been very different. I know that."

"So what exactly are you trying to tell us. That you contributed to Heywood's inventions?" asked Cortland.

"In a way definitely yes, I contributed, but never got credit, I never got thanked, I just got treated badly."

"So I got frustrated," he continued. "By then I just wanted to get to him, do something to make sure I got to him, get his attention. The only way I figured I could get anyone's attention was to write a note like that." He let that sit in the air for awhile, shrugged his shoulders and said, "Well, looks like it might have worked, doesn't it."

REUNION

Cortland had visited with Heywood and told him who they picked up and why. He was now known as Robert Rega, but it had been easy for them to find out that he had originally been Tony Camera from Flushing, Queens, New York, the same town where Heywood grew up.

"I'm in shock, needless to say I'm in shock. I knew this man when he was a young boy. He was a good kid. He was a good friend to me. How can this be?" Heywood asked Cortland.

"I don't know. You don't know what happens inside of people sometimes," Cortland answered.

"This will be the first time we've seen each other or spoken to each other since we were I think thirteen years old. This is bizarre, at best," Heywood said, deep in thought. "I can't believe he would want to threaten me. I can't make it make sense. He was always only kind and protective of me."

Now Cortland and Heywood sat in one of the rooms just outside the cell holding area. They selected the one with the cushioned couch and comfortable chairs, at Heywood's insistence, to avoid the appearance of a cold prison for their first meeting in so many years.

There was a guard standing against the far

wall. Also at Heywood's insistence, Rega had been allowed to keep on the clothing that he was detained in so that he could feel some level of dignity, so that he would talk more.

Soon another guard walked Rega into the room. When he and Heywood saw each other, Heywood asked Cortland and the guards if it would be all right for him to hug his old friend. They said yes, and he did that.

"My old friend Tony. Tony Camera. I thought I would never see you again. I am so sorry that we are seeing each other here," Heywood said.

The guards were ready to pounce if their charge even winced. But he didn't. Instead he started to sob, ever so softly.

"Let's all sit down," Cortland said. And with that, they all sat on the cushion seats and stared at each other.

"Why are we here, why are you here, what happened, Tony," Heywood asked.

"It's good to see you Douggie. It's really good to see you." Rega, said. "I've been a jerk," he continued. "Remember when we were kids, I had a terrible temper."

"Yes, I do remember that," answered Heywood. "But it seemed then, even at that young age, that you knew how to use it, and how to channel it. You most certainly used it to save me more than once. And for that I have always wanted to thank you."

Rega stared at him with disbelief. "Since my parents died and I was taken from the neighborhood, that's all I ever wanted to hear."

"So what are you doing here," Heywood asked him, as if he were scolding a child. "If you had only gotten in touch with me the right way," Heywood continued, "I would have gladly told you how much our childhood friendship meant to me."

He paused, he needed to think, to remember. Then he continued, "But I didn't know where you were after you left the neighborhood, and then the years just went by. How sad this all is. You meant so much to me then."

"I held a grudge. I felt slighted, my whole life I felt slighted. It was always one thing or another. You were the symbol of it."

He paused, "It's not that my life suffered, later I did good, I've been living large, I have a beautiful wife, I have money, a great house. But I've carried around this piss show all these years. What a waste."

"But when I tried to call different government departments, they wouldn't look for you for me, they wouldn't even try." Heywood and Cortland knew that the State Department truly had no idea how to find him.

Cortland and Heywood understood that they were purposefully being extra kind to this man so that they could get more information from him. Like what did he have to do with Amy's kidnapping.

"I still don't really understand," Heywood said. "I'm considered a genius in the world, but this situation is only confusing to me."

"Simple. You wanna know the truth, here's the truth. I didn't think you could have gotten this far if it hadn't been for me protecting you. I never got thanked, I never got glory. Is it so wrong to want some of that? I helped you help the world. That's how I see it."

All I had, Rega thought, were my goof ball men who worked for me. All so low level compared to Heywood's life.

"You know it cost us millions of dollars to find this out from you," Cortland told him. They all looked at him, trying to hide their fury.

"Truth is, as kinda dumb as it sounds now, I was just pissed. Trying to act the big shot to my wife, but really I was always just hustling, my whole life I've been hustling, I'm just a hustler. I just wanted some more higher level credit for something." He looked down and admitted, "I guess I didn't really think through what I was setting in motion. I guess I really am that dumb."

I am just a hustler, Rega thought to himself.

He felt defeated, tired, like the loser he always thought he was but dressed in fine clothing. My Cara, my Cara, I just want to go home to her.

"Can I call my wife," Rega asked. "She's gotta be worried about me. I shoulda been home by now."

"Sure you can, in a few minutes, but we're not finished here yet," Cortland said. After a minutes pause he locked his eyes in Rega's eyes and asked, "Why did you kidnap and torture that girl," hoping the element of surprise would take advantage of his vulnerable mood.

"What girl? What are you talking about?" Rega responded.

There was no sign of recognition there. By the look on Rega's face, Cortland no longer thought that Rega had to do with Amy's kidnapping. But if it wasn't Rega's doing, who took her, and why?

I'M METICULOUS

I'm meticulous. That's why they never find me. Nobody is cleaner, they always said you could eat off my floor. I use drug store rubbing alcohol to clean everything, I leave no residue. That's why they hire me, to keep things neat, to keep things clean, to keep things organized. I can't help it I hate messes and filth.

What would I do if they found me, I'd deny it, I'd deny every bit of it.

I saw a headline today. Seems hair falls out of your scalp, not just on your brush or comb or in the shower. So, only my hairdresser would know it's mine how could anyone else know it's mine.

CARA NEEDS TO SHOP

It was nice to be back from Florida. And Cara so loved her home. But her Rega was beginning to worry her. He was staying out later with his men again. Nothing was making sense. Who in the world was he after and why.

She had made a lunch date with Cerise, her favorite shopping partner. Because Cerise had a way of hearing things.

TOO MUCH

They let him call Cara. He hadn't been sure what he was going to say to her. Her voicemail picked up so he just left a message saying that he was running late, maybe would have to stay out of town over night for a business meeting, would call her later or in the morning, depending on how late things ran. He'd done that before, that should hold things for now. He could live with that message cause he knew she could.

What is going to happen to me now. He needed to calm down. He didn't want to lose his life.

Alone in his holding room in the facility, Rega remembered his run in with Frank those months ago, his insane employee friend Frank, who only wanted to please him, show him how good and faithful he was, do extra things for him all the time, show him he was always on the case.

But Frank was trouble. Rega met him when he moved with his aunt and uncle when he was thirteen years old. He had taken Frank under his wing because he always needed someone to be a front for him if he had something going, like when he was running numbers or when he owned all the bets on Long Island. Frank ran for him, delivered messages, delivered money without knowing that's what he was doing. He was good, he was faithful, he always did everything I asked him to do.

But he was trouble because he was even more out of his mind than I ever was, Rega thought. I can't let them think that was me. I can't protect Frank now. If he had the girl they're talking about, he's going down, and I'm not going with him. Sorry old pal, but I told you then and I'll tell you now, what you did was worse than anything I ever did.

HE DIDN'T COME HOME

When Rega didn't come home that night, she didn't think that much of it, it had happened before, those business meetings of his. Especially if they were drinking with their business dinner, she wouldn't have wanted him home anyway, smelling like he was drinking with the boys and smoking cigars. But Rega had been behaving so strangely lately, could this have something to do with that.

What to have for dinner. Where's Belinda, I don't even know if she's working today. "Belinda," she called. "Belinda, where are you?"

She didn't have time to change, she was wearing her day off clothes.

"Mrs. Rega, Mrs. Rega, I'm here, what do you want?"

"I'm getting hungry for dinner, Belinda. Can we make something please?"

"Of course, Mrs. Rega. What do you feel like having?"

"Whatever is easy to make, I'm hungry, I'll be right there."

Cara came down the stairs and walked into the kitchen. She hardly recognized Belinda. "Where have you been, you look a mess, Belinda."

I better think fast, she thought. "Oh, I've

been working out and jogging. You're right, I'm a mess. I didn't have a chance to shower yet."

"Oh no wonder you're wearing work out clothes. Well, that's good that you work out, that's good."

Belinda was wearing her black stretch pants, long sleeve black tee shirt and black sneakers, sort of like what everyone wears at the gym, she thought.

"Where is Mr. Rega tonight, will he be having dinner with you too?" she asked.

"He has a late meeting tonight, probably drinking with the men after, so he'll be home later or tomorrow. So right now it's just you and me."

"That's nice, Mrs. Rega, that's nice. Would you like pasta and clams?"

"That's perfect, Belinda. Thank you."

Belinda didn't usually cook for them, she wasn't a chef, but she could put together something simple. Of course Cara would rather go out to eat or just heat up one of the gourmet prepared meals that were always in the freezer. But she was glad for the company tonight. She was getting frightened.

HAIRS

She saw the headlines and she didn't like it, she didn't understand it, she didn't know what to do about it. What were they talking about anyway. Hairs. They were talking about hairs. The headline said hairs were found at crime scenes. What crime scenes, could they be more specific please.

They said they didn't want to be more specific because they didn't want to give away more than they had to.

They could at least say which particular crime scenes, couldn't they?

All she knew is that they were testing the hairs they were finding. So what, what can they tell by that, if the hair is from a person or a dog or a chimpanzee. Big deal. As long as I'm still here and they're still there, who cares.

Did they find anything else besides hairs, like footprints, or handprints, or what. Really, what was there to find except some really beautiful designs, what else mattered.

IF I GIVE IT UP TO YOU

If I give it up to them, will it save me. That's all he could think about all night. Rega was so used to the comforts of his home, his cars, his wife, his clothes, their travels. Even the boys, his crazy boys, they were nuts, but they did good work for him. Except for one of them.

He and Cara had it all, and he made sure of it, even when providing it all meant playing some games. But they were business games, they didn't hurt anyone. It was just knowing how to trade, knowing how to bargain, knowing how to make sure the business came to you and not the other guy. That's it, that's the whole thing.

I gotta get some sleep. I can tell that tomorrow is going to be one of the heaviest days of my life and I have to be able to do it right.

CARA'S PHONE

Cara's phone was ringing. She was already waking up. It was nine in the morning. Who could be calling, she didn't recognize the number. In her not totally up yet sleepiness she thought that maybe it was where Rega is staying, so he was using the hotel phone. So she answered.

"Hello, good morning dear," she said.

It was a man's voice but it wasn't Rega's.

"Hello, is this Mrs. Rega?"

She almost hung up, probably one of those scam calls, but who calls so early, and who knows our name.

"Who is this?" she insisted.

"Really sorry to bother you so early, ma'am. This is an assistant at the Motor Vehicle Bureau, in Nassau County. We have a license application here, from a Miss Belinda Banner, with your address. Since she isn't otherwise listed at your address, we wanted to call to verify that she lives there and that she is authorized to use your address."

"Well, that's a surprise Mr. ah..."

"Oh sorry, this is Mr. Jackson from the Motor Vehicle Bureau for Nassau County. Sorry to bother you so early in the morning, but we have a backlog of applications here that we are trying to get through."

283

"I understand." She didn't really, but she wanted to be helpful and figure this out. She did think Belinda had her own apartment, her own address, she didn't know she needed to use our address, she thought.

"Mr. Jackson. Can I have your number please, and I'll call you back."

"Yes, of course, Mrs. Rega. Thank you for your help with this."

WAKE UP WAKE UP

It's eight in the morning. Rega was woken by a knock on the door and a breakfast tray of coffee, cereal, eggs, and orange juice.

At nine o'clock, Cortland and Brenner walked in to his cell room, followed by Colter and Grange who sat off to the side.

For the next two hours he was questioned again about his years growing up with Heywood, all the years since then, and his crazy stupid move trying to get Heywood's attention. His stories were consistent with yesterday.

Then they asked him about Amy's kidnapping again. This time he gave them what they needed.

That afternoon, Frank was picked up at his house and questioned about Amy's kidnapping. With the threat of worse than a life in hell, Frank gave them the names of everyone who had been in the house during that time.

They had to hold Cortland back, he wanted to kill him.

PROTECT ME

Cara really would have liked to spend another day shopping with Cerise, it was relaxing. There seemed to be so much pressure around everything lately. Rega still wasn't home, and he hadn't called yet today.

The only information she had been able to get out of Cerise was that she thought that the men were trying to come up with some new business ventures, so there was tension in the air. Cerise said she heard her husband on the phone with Elliot the other night, and it sounded like he might be having a problem with an oversees customer. Things like that always put a strain in the air, she thought. She hadn't heard about anything else.

The doorbell rang. The doorbell rang? Who got past the guards? Why aren't the dogs barking?

Paul, who Rega liked to call Pepper, answered the door then went running down the hall to Mrs. Rega. "Mrs. Rega," he said. "There are two men here. They say they are from the New York City police department."

"What?" Cara said. "Where are the guards, Paul? How did they get to the front door? Are you sure they are really policemen?" she asked, as she walked with him to the door.

"Stay with me Paul, please, stay right here with me while I see what this is."

When she got to the door there were two men, both dressed cheap preppy but clean and okay. She introduced herself and asked what they wanted.

"I'm Detective Colter, and this is Detective Grange. Sorry to barge in on you like this, but this is an important police matter."

She looked skeptical, so they showed her their badges and ID, and explained that her guards had no choice but to let them in.

"I'm sure my husband can help you with whatever it is that you're doing," she said. "But I'm sorry, he's not home right now." Then she added, just to make herself feel more secure, "but he'll be home any minute now."

They knew he wouldn't be home any minute now.

Colter spoke in as low a tone as he could. "Mrs. Rega, do you have a young lady working here who calls herself Belinda Banner?"

"Well, yes I do. Why would you ask me that?"

"We need to talk to her. Right now. She might be in a little bit of trouble."

"What? What are you talking about? Belinda has worked for us for years, she's terrific, she organizes everything for us. What in the world could you want with her?"

"I'm sorry, we are not at liberty to tell you that. But we do need to talk to her. Right now." He paused and then added, "We don't have much time, Mrs. Rega."

"Well, alright, if you need to speak with her, then of course you should speak to her and straighten whatever it is out. I'll get her for you."

"Please Mrs. Rega, stay right here and just call for her. Please just do it that way for us."

"Belinda. Belinda, could you come down here please," she shouted.

And exactly five beats later, they heard the back door slam and then heard someone running off in the back of the house rustling the leaves.

Grange took off after her. A few minutes later he had her, handcuffed and crying.

"Mrs. Rega, what are they doing to me. Mrs. Rega," Belinda pleaded.

"Belinda, don't worry. I'm sure there has been a mistake. I'll have Mr. Rega help you as soon as he gets home. Don't worry about anything."

And with that, Belinda flipped out and started to scream out of control, "That's exactly what he promised me. That he would always take care of me, he promised. He promised to protect me from everything. And then he went away. He disappeared. He left me to live by myself, I could never do it right. That's why I got a job with you. To be near him. To feel safe again. But he didn't know it was me. Why did he leave me?" she sobbed. "Why did he leave me?"

"What is going on here officer, what in the world is going on here?" Cara implored.

"We'll have someone explain it to you today, I promise Mrs. Rega. In the meantime, we have to take her in for questioning."

Cara was left standing there with her mouth agape and her understanding of her every day life in a haze of peril.

COUNTING ON YOU

"Sounds like you had a lot of people counting on you, Tony." Rega wasn't sure what Heywood was talking about, but he sat there and listened, unsure what his future would be. He was probably going to be spending the rest of his life in prison. He knew he deserved it.

Who else knew he was Tony but his old friend Douglas Heywood. To him I would always be Tony, thought Rega, and to me he would always be Douggie.

Heywood and Rega were having coffee and pie in one of the private lounges of the Federal Building. They were waiting to be joined by Cortland, Colter and Grange. Everybody poured themselves coffee from the silver urn into coffee cups that had a golden orb circled with a gold and silver ring on the side. It was a beautiful logo that long ago was willed by a wealthy benefactor who had immigrated to the United States decades before, having escaped much suffering, and here became a noted hotelier who wanted the government that he loved to have beautiful sets of china that bore the symbol of the jewelry of his grandmother who he so loved.

The Feds had issued Rega pajamas and clean underwear, and in one hour they had dry-cleaned his clothing so he felt a little better.

"Rega," Heywood continued. "This has been a terrible time for us all, each for our own reasons. Cortland might have some news for you when he arrives."

Just then the door opened and Cortland walked in with Colter and Grange. They all walked with purposeful energy as if they had a lot to talk about and resolve.

Cortland started. "Listen Rega, I abhor the way you behaved, I am furious that you were so thoughtless sending that frightening letter to Heywood. You caused much confusion, you came close to causing an international incident, and you did cause so much fear."

Rega felt terrible. He really did. He looked around the room and didn't say anything but the sorrow was on his face.

Cortland continued, "And much money was spent to find out that, after all, it was you, carrying around an old grudge like a turtle lugging around a shell on his back for his whole life. But you did that by choice." He really was trying to calm his fury, he took a few deep breaths and continued, "But if Heywood is willing to forgive you for putting his family through hell, then I will forgive you that too."

Rega looked around the room, first to Cortland, then to Heywood, and couldn't help but say that he was moved more than he could say by this.

They all raised their coffee cups and said here here.

But Cortland had more to say. "While we are still on this subject, Rega, I think Heywood wants to say something around now."

"Tony. Rega. Whatever you want me to call you. I've been hurt more than you can know by this, and I've also been touched more than I can say. But I realize it's important for me that you are in my life again. I want it to stay that way."

Rega had a look of utter bewilderment on his face. He had been expecting jail and a life sentence. He was slow processing all that he was hearing.

"You are surely still the same rough around the edges Tony that you were then, but I knew it then, and I know it now, that you have a good heart, you don't mean harm, you really do want to help. And so I have some work that I would like to discuss with you. That would involve working with me, if that is something that might appeal to you."

"Wow Douggie, I didn't expect that. I really didn't." Rega was beginning to feel like it was his birthday, this was beyond words.

"But we'll talk about that later." Heywood continued, "I think Cortland has a little more to say to you."

They passed around the breakfast rolls and each poured a little more coffee.

"Rega. You know, I am madly in love with a woman named Amy. I have loved her for some time. She was kidnapped, raped and tortured by someone you know. But you had the decency to stop it when you did, soon as you knew of it, and you turned him in to us when you realized the reality of the connection. We have him now, he's in custody, and I promise the world that he will never get out. For that I am grateful to you."

"I am mortified that someone I know did that to someone you love. I don't know what else to say about it right now. I am just glad I was able to put a stop to it, and I am glad that he is getting what he deserves for what he did."

They all raised their coffee cups again.

"I know you would like to go home now, Rega, and see your wife and your house again. But there is more," Heywood offered.

Rega was befuddled. This was already too much, what else could there be, he wondered.

"Rega, do you remember a girl from our childhood named Rita Banner?" Heywood asked him.

Rega thought about it for a few seconds, and then said, "yes, I do, I do remember that name. Why in the world would you bring her up now?" he asked.

"I think we'll let Colter and Grange fill you in on this part," Cortland answered.

Colter began by asking, "Mr. Rega, have you been reading the local papers, and seeing local news. About some recent murders?"

"There are always murders in this area, and we always hear about murders in this country. Why are you asking me that?" Rega wondered.

"Well," Colter continued, "I'm asking specifically about the murders that have been written about that involved carvings on the victim's bodies. Did you hear about any of those?"

"Well, of course I did. How can you help it living here. There were a number of them, they were talked about on the news a lot."

"Well, you better stay sitting down," Colter said, as he looked around at everyone's expectant faces.

"We arrested the perp today," Colter continued. "And it's someone you know."

"It's someone I know? Are you kidding me? Why would I know someone like that? That's a crazy thing to say to me," Rega insisted.

"Do you know someone named Belinda Banner?" Grange asked him.

"Well of course I do, I'm sure you know I do, she's a sweet girl that helps me and my wife around the house. She does our errands, goes food shopping, takes our things to the cleaners, keeps our things organized, things like that. She's really great." Then he stopped to think and said, "Wait a minute, did something happen to her? What are you telling me? Is she okay? Cara is alone in the house with her and our helper Paul. Did something happen to Belinda?"

"No," Cortland said. "Nothing happened to Belinda, she's fine." He paused, and then added, "Well, she's not actually fine. She is in custody right now."

"She's where? Why?" Rega asked.

"We determined that she was the black flower murderer."

Rega was stunned. He couldn't move. Then he said, "What are you telling me, this sweet girl is a murderer? I had a murderer living under the same roof as me and my Cara? I'm having a problem with what you're saying."

Colter said, "When Grange and I arrested her, all she did was scream that when she was a little girl you had promised to protect her. But then you left. And that's why years later she found you and got a job working for you. The only place in the world that she said she felt safe is if she was near you."

"Where's my Cara," Rega asked. "Is Cara okay?"

"Yes, your Cara is fine. I'm sure she's in shock as you are," Grange said.

"Every time she killed someone, she would leave a note that said My Name Is Rita," Colter said.

"We found bodies in New York City, in Florida and in Cannes," Cortland added. "She was prolific. She is insane."

"I remember her," Heywood said. "I remember her clearly. She was a cute little girl but she was afraid of everything. Like me, she turned to you for strength and protection." Then he thought about it for a minute and added, "I remember that you and I thought she had a lot of problems. Even at that young age we knew it. But who could have imagined this madness."

"I don't know what to make of it," Rega said. "I just want to know that my Cara is okay."

"Looks like you had more people depending on you than you ever knew, Mr. Rega," said Cortland.

"I want to say that these last forty-eight hours have been shocking. I want to say that I think I've never been so tired in my life."

"You probably just want to go home now," Heywood said.

"Yes, I do. I just want to go home now." Rega said. He looked around the room at each man. "I just want to thank you all for this day."

Rega and Heywood said they would speak again in a day or two, after everyone had a chance to rest.

"Blackbird and black flowers," Cortland thought. What a coincidence.

Made in the USA
Las Vegas, NV
20 August 2021